The Promise

SILVINA OCAMPO

Translated by
Suzanne Jill Levine
and Jessica Powell

City Lights Books | San Francisco

First published in Spanish as *La promesa* in 2010.

This work was published with the sponsorship of the "Sur" Translation
Support Program administered by the Argentine Republic's Ministry of
Foreign Affairs and Worship. / *Obra editada en el marco del Programa "Sur" de Apoyo a
las Traducciones del Ministerio de Relaciones Exteriores y Culto de la República Argentina.*

Cover photo of Silvina Ocampo by Pepe Fernández, courtesy of
Mariana G. Fernández of @archivo_pepefernandez
Cover design by Elizabeth Knafo/Noctiluna Design

Library of Congress Cataloging-in-Publication Data

Names: Ocampo, Silvina, author. | Levine, Suzanne Jill, translator. |
    Powell, Jessica, translator.
Title: The promise / Silvina Ocampo ; translated by Suzanne Jill Levine and
    Jessica Powell.
Other titles: Promesa. English
Description: San Francisco : City Lights Books, [2019] | Translated into
English from Spanish. | Summary: "A dying woman's attempt to recount the
story of her life reveals the fragility of memory and the illusion of identity"—
Provided by publisher.
Identifiers: LCCN 2019027247 (print) | LCCN 2019027248 (ebook) | ISBN
    9780872867710 (paperback) | ISBN 9780872868038 (ebook)
Classification: LCC PQ7797.O293 P7613 2019 (print) | LCC PQ7797.
O293
    (ebook) | DDC 863/.64—dc23
LC record available at https://lccn.loc.gov/2019027247
LC ebook record available at https://lccn.loc.gov/2019027248

City Lights Books are published at the City Lights Bookstore
261 Columbus Avenue, San Francisco, CA 94133
www.citylights.com

"Silvina Ocampo's prose is made of elegant pleasures and delicate terrors. Her stories take place in a liquid, viscous reality, where innocence quietly bleeds into cruelty, and the mundane seeps, unnoticed, into the bizarre. Revered by some of the masters of fantastic literature, such as Italo Calvino and Jorge Luis Borges, Ocampo is beyond great—she is necessary."—**Hernan Diaz, author of *In the Distance* and Associate Director of the Hispanic Institute at Columbia University**

"A woman examines her life piecemeal, putting it together like a puzzle missing half its pieces—but the resulting image is all the more mesmerizing because of it. A deft and subtle novel that holds together as airily as a spider's web."—**Brian Evenson, author of *Song for the Unraveling of the World: Stories***

"Silvina Ocampo's *The Promise*, which she spent 25 years perfecting, is one of my favorite books of 2019. It's one of the most hopeful novels I've read in a long time, about the necessity of storytelling and the power of the mind."—**Gabe Habash, author of *Stephen Florida***

"Only a masterful storyteller could pull off what Silvina Ocampo does in *The Promise;* a woman lost at sea drowns in her memories, while the water—never threatening—cradles her with echoes of the past. A novel that is not a novel; a hypnosis, really."—**Gabriela Alemán, author of *Poso Wells***

"Translated into English for the first time by Suzanne Jill Levine, one of Latin America's most gifted translators, and Jessica Powell, *The Promise* brings to an English-speaking public the work of Silvina Ocampo, a writer of great depth and audacity. *The Promise,* a novel written and rewritten over a period of 25 years, recounts the story of a woman adrift at sea telling and remembering her own life as well as the lives of others. An exquisite, fantastical, and philosophical novel that dwells on the ways one represents a life without fears or conventions. A masterpiece from an extraordinary author who deserves to be read over and over. A gem."—**Marjorie Agosín, author of *I Lived On Butterfly Hill***

"This haunting and vital final work from Ocampo (1903–1993), her only novel, is about a woman's life flashing before her eyes when she's stranded in the ocean. The nameless narrator has fallen off a ship, and as she floats, her mind takes over, presenting a flotilla of real and imagined memories about the people in her life in the form of a version of the book she promises herself she'll finish. The book's main thread is a woman, Irene, and a man, Leandro, with whom both Irene and the narrator get involved. But the fluid narrative also encompasses brief snapshots of a murder mystery, the narrator's grandmother's eye doctor ('In profile, his intent rabbit face was not as kind as it was head-on.'), her hairdresser, her ballerina neighbor, and the fruit vendor to whom her brother was attracted as a boy ('it was a fruit relationship, perhaps symbolizing sex'). The narrator's potent, dynamic voice yields countless memorable lines and observations: 'The only advantage of being a child is that time is doubly wide, like upholstery fabric'; 'What is falling in love, anyway? Letting go of disgust, of fear, letting go of everything.' But the book's true power is its depiction of the strength of the mind ('what I imagine becomes real, more real than reality') and the necessity of storytelling, which for the narrator is literally staving off death: 'I told stories to death so that it would spare my life.' Ocampo's portrait of one woman's interior life is forceful and full of hope."— ***Publishers Weekly*, * Starred Review**

"Silvina Ocampo's richly textured world shimmers with childhood sweetness and sorrow. Her narrator's hyper-observant gaze travels through the multiplying interiors of houses, mirrors, dresses, adult giants, dream figures, and nimble acrobats, in search of love stolen by bad magic. Ocampo inhabits and brings to life a hyperreal, surreal, and resolutely feminine world ruled by unapologetic beauty and pervading sadness. She is a close kin of Remedios Varo and Frida Kahlo, weavers of the magical Latin American art that bewitches us time after time. This beautiful translation fully renders that magic."—**Andrei Codrescu, author of *No Time Like Now: New Poems***

"Silvina Ocampo's fiction is wondrous, heart-piercing, and fiercely strange. Her fabulism is as charming as Borges's. Her restless sense of invention foregrounds the brilliant feminist work of writers like Clarice Lispector and Samanta Schweblin. It's thrilling to have work of this magnitude finally translated into English, head-spinning and thrilling."—**Alyson Hagy, author of *Scribe***

"There is literature that takes the known world (a dinner party or a walk with a dog, first love or a visit to friends) and shows it in a way we've never seen before; there is literature that takes us to a place we've never been (early twentieth-century Buenos Aires or adrift in the middle of the ocean) and makes it somehow familiar. The marvel of Silvina Ocampo's fiction is that it does both things simultaneously, its deepest context the confluence of the things of this world ('a heavy wool dress embroidered with flowers, the sleeves poorly attached,' 'a big box full of nails, newspaper clippings and old pieces of wire,' 'vanity tables without legs . . . old pharmaceutical flasks . . . chess pieces, chandeliers, minatures') and the ineffable mystery of mortality ('I close the windows, shut my eyes and see blue, green, red, yellow, purple, white, white. White foam, blue. Death will be like this, when it drags me from the little room of my hands.')"—**Kathryn Davis, author of *The Silk Road***

"Silvina Ocampo was once called the 'the best kept secret of Argentine letters,' and was, through her own work and that of those she championed, a key figure of modernism. Known primarily in the English-speaking world as a friend of Borges and wife to his collaborator Bioy Casares, the translation of two more of her works into English is a reason to celebrate her in her own right, as one of the most singular writers of the 20th century."—**Stephen Sparks, Point Reyes Books, CA**

Year by year, more of the great Argentinian Silvina Ocampo is restored to us, like the lost work of a luminously dark seer. Borges and Calvino were in her thrall: the fantastic Mariana Enriquez has written an entire book on her. Yet Ocampo remains an obscure writer to most. Yet what work she wrote, what an incredible life she lived. These two newly translated books could make her a rediscovery on par with Clarice Lispector. In *The Promise*, a woman falls overboard a transatlantic ship and confronts her regrets and longings as she bobs in the freezing water. *Forgotten Journey* gives us 28 short stories, translated into English for the first time, providing a surprising glimpse of the birth of gothic fiction in Latin America, which dates back to the 1930s. Lusciously strange, uncompromising, yet balanced and precise, there has never been another voice like hers."—**John Freeman, Executive Editor, *LITHUB***

"Silvina Ocampo is one of our best writers. Her stories have no equal in our literature."—**Jorge Luis Borges**

"I don't know of another writer who better captures the magic inside everyday rituals, the forbidden or hidden face that our mirrors don't show us."—**Italo Calvino**

"Like William Blake, Ocampo's first voice was that of a visual artist; in her writing she retains the will to unveil immaterial so that we might at least look at it if not touch it."—**Helen Oyeyemi, author of _Gingerbread_**

"A woman relives the people and places of her life while stranded in the middle of the ocean. The premise of Argentinian writer Ocampo's posthumously published novella, which she worked on for the final 25 years of her life, is a grand metaphor for the authorial condition. On her way to visit family in Cape Town, the nameless narrator somehow slips over the railing of her transatlantic ship and regains consciousness in the water, watching 'the ship...calmly moving away.' Adrift, facing almost certain death, she makes a pact with St. Rita, the 'arbiter of the impossible,' that she will write a 'dictionary of memories,' and publish it in one year's time, if she is saved. What follows is an intensely focused series of vignettes in which the characters of the narrator's life once more walk through their dramas. There's Leandro, a handsome and feckless young doctor with 'a face as variable as the weather'; Irene, his intensely focused lover and a medical student in her own right; Gabriela, Irene's obsessive daughter; and Verónica, a not-so-innocent ingénue. These central characters' stories entwine and begin to form the basis of a tale that includes our narrator—who is present as a voyeur but never an active participant—but her drifting consciousness is just as likely to alight upon less crucial secondary characters like Worm, Gabriela's countryside companion, or Lily and Lillian, devoted friends who fall in love with the same man because 'instead of kissing him they were kissing each other.' As the narrator's memories progress, and sometimes repeat, they grow increasingly nightmarish in their domestic surrealism. Meanwhile, as all chance of rescue fades, her sense of self is diluted by the immense mystery of the sea. Completed in the late 1980s, at a time when Ocampo was grappling with the effects of Alzheimer's, the book can be read as a treatise on the dissolution of selfhood in the face of the disease. However, its tactile insistence on the recurrence of memory, its strangeness, and its febrile reality are themes that mark the entirety of Ocampo's oeuvre and articulate something more enduring even than death. 'I'm going to die soon! If I die before I finish what I'm writing no one will remember me, not even the person I loved most in the world,' the narrator exclaims in the final pages. This urgency and despair seem to sum up the central tenet of the artist's condition—even in the final extreme, the act of making is a tonic against obscurity. Art is the cure for death. A seminal work by an underread master. Required for all students of the human condition." —*Kirkus Reviews*, * **Starred Review**

The Promise

It is painful to finish something. Why mark it like Beethoven, who wastes five full minutes on final chords? His whole oeuvre is impregnated with that final concern. I don't like conventions, that a novel need have an ending, for example.

S.O. to Noemi Ulla
Encounters with Silvina Ocampo (1982)

Between 1988 and 1989, besieged by the illness that would darken the last years of her life, Silvina Ocampo laboriously devoted herself to correcting and finishing *The Promise*, the novel she had been working on sporadically since the mid 1960s.[1] During that long period of almost twenty-five years, she had gone through several cycles of writing, abandoning and resuming once again her work on this book. Nevertheless, its existence as "work-in-progress" was never completely secret, at least beginning late in 1966, when it had been announced in a brief journalistic note stating that Silvina Ocampo "is

---

1. The earliest draft that has been found, titled "En la orilla del sueño" ("On the Shores of Sleep"), is preserved in a notebook where there are also sketches of poems from *Amarillo celeste* (*Sky Blue Yellow*, 1972) and a letter in which the author refers to the death of her husband's father, Adolfo Bioy, which occurred in August 1962.

currently working on a novel which still does not have a definitive title."[2]

In 1975, in response to an epistolary questionnaire, the author revealed one of her preliminary titles for the novel—"The Epicenes"—declaring that it was "the best I've ever written" and stating that "according to my calculations it will be finished by the end of next year."[3] In an interview published three years later, she described it as a "phantasmagorical novel" and confessed the difficulty she was having in trying to finish it "because the main character is endlessly telling us things; something is making this woman talk on and on, telling one thing after another. It's a promise she has made and that she keeps so as not to die, but one can tell she is dying."[4] This brief summary of her plot provides a key to reading *The Promise* under the guise of a posthumous autobiography and at the same time anticipates, with tragic irony, the conclusion that would join in a similar fate, ten years later, the main character and her author.

The Promise is the longest work of fiction by Silvina Ocampo, hence demanding of her, to judge by the numerous preliminary versions, a greater compositional effort. Structured as a series of linked stories, it takes its form as a "dictionary of memories" that the nameless

---

2. "Vida literaria" ("Literary Life") *La Nación*, October 9, 1966

3. Danubio Torres Fierro, "Correspondencia con Silvina Ocampo (Una Entrevista Que No Osa Decir Su Nombre)" ("Correspondence with Silvina Ocampo (An Interview That Dares Not Speak Its Name"), *Plural*, no. 50, November 1975, pp. 57-60.

4. María Esther Vázquez, "Con Silvina Ocampo" ("With Silvina Ocampo,") *La Nación*, September 10, 1978.

narrator recounts as she is dying, drifting in the ocean after falling off the ship on which she was traveling. The persons she knew throughout her life parade, erratically, through the theater of her memory, many of them receiving only a brief biographical sketch that, for the most part, becomes an autonomous story, complete unto itself. Others belong to a continuous single story whose branches cover most of the novel. Her choice of this concentric structure, open to multiple digressions and interpolations, is not surprising in one who asserted that she had chosen the short story form "out of impatience" and who made a literary creed of concision and brevity. Freed of the constraints that a linear development would have imposed upon her, she could devote herself to the independent and concentrated invention of episodes, which could then be inserted in the text without altering the proliferating architecture of the whole. Nevertheless, those alternating narrative levels doubtlessly required an intricate embroidery of episodes—which helps to explain the novel's point-counterpoint movements—and also necessitated the arduous process of writing she sustained.

Over the years, during this prolonged labor of editing and assembling, *The Promise* underwent at least two substantial modifications. The first was the extraction of sixteen of its episodes, which the author included as stories in the volume *Los días de la noche* (*The Days of Night*, 1970)[5], although she included one of them, "Livio Roca," in both works. Shortly afterward, she undertook a labyrinthine story of discordant passions among two women, a man,

---

5. They are the following: "Ulises," "Atínganos," "Las esclavas de las criadas,"

and a young girl, whose features and man's name—the archangelic "Gabriel"—appear to have given rise to the discarded title *epicene.*[6] This story, from a screenplay written in the mid '50s entitled *Amor desencontrado (Misencountered Love)*, is the only one the narrator takes up again, circuitously, throughout the course of her tale.

The present text is the last version of *The Promise* found among the author's papers. The manuscript, in a file folder with the definitive title on its front cover, consists of 152 typewritten pages, upon which there are a few scattered corrections and additions in Silvina Ocampo's own hand. As with the majority of the author's manuscripts, this text was typed up by Elena Ivulich, her secretary for more than forty years. As a general rule, we have only altered the author's syntax or punctuation when it was necessary in order to assure the full legibility of the text; in a few instances, however, it was necessary to consult the earlier drafts—handwritten and typed—in order to resolve transcription errors. At the same time, it's worth clarifying that the repetition of some scenes, with slight variations in the narrator's point of view or in the characters' identities, adheres to the novel's plan, as evidenced by a note handwritten by Ivulich, inserted among the pages of the manuscript, in which she indicates the location within the text of some of these re-writings and adds that they are deliberate because "the memories are recurrent."

"Ana Valerga," "El enigma," "Celestino Abril," "La soga," "Coral Fernández," "Livio Roca," "Clavel," "Albino Orma," "Clotilde Ifrán," "Malva," "Amancio Luna, el sacerdote," "La divina," "Paradela," and "Carl Herst."

6. Another of the preliminary titles was *Memoria de la ciudad perdida* (*Memoir of the Lost City*).

Independent of her declared aversion to endings governed by literary convention, the author did not leave precise indications that could confirm whether or not she considered *The Promise* finished. Nevertheless, the vertiginous dissolution of the narrator's consciousness, recorded in the last stretch of the novel with increasing lyrical exuberance, corresponds to the author's succinct description of its phantasmagorical plot. Those final pages of *The Promise*, written by hand on loose sheets of paper, with intricate and faltering strokes, are also some of Silvina Ocampo's final pages. In them the author and her protagonist appear to share, at moments, the same voice.

Ernesto Montequín
Translator, literary critic, and director
of the Villa Ocampo Center in Buenos Aires

The Promise

I'm such an ignoramus. How could I think of publishing this text! What publisher would accept it? I think it would be impossible, it would take a miracle. Though I do believe in miracles.

"I love you and promise to be a good girl," I used to tell her when I was a child, so that she would feel sympathy for me, and for a long time afterward whenever I'd ask her for a favor, until I learned she was famous for being an "arbiter of the impossible." There are people who don't understand that you speak to a saint as you would to anybody. If they'd known all my prayers they'd say they were sacrilegious and that I am not a devout believer in Saint Rita.

Statues and figurines usually depict this saint holding a mysterious wooden book in her hand, which she rests against her heart. I had not forgotten the detail of this pose when I made her the promise that, if I were saved, I would write this book and finish it by the time my next birthday rolled around. That date is almost a year away. I've begun to feel anxious. I knew it would be a great sacrifice to keep my promise. To create this dictionary of memories that are at times shameful, even humiliating, would mean revealing my intimate world to anyone and everyone. (Perhaps this anxiety was unfounded.)

I don't have a life of my own; I have only feelings. My experiences were never important—not during the course of my life nor even on the threshold of death. Instead, the lives of others have become mine.

Typing up these pages would be an arduous task, since I don't have the money to pay a typist, nor any altruistic friends who know how to type. Presenting the manuscript to editors, or to any publisher in the world who might refuse to publish the book, would mean sacrificing my sense of pride, since I would then be obliged to pay for publishing it with the sale of objects I value or with some menial work, the only kind of work I can do.

How distant are those happy days in Palermo with my little nephews playing on the swings and the slide, eating dime-store chocolates or chewy white taffy. Those times when I felt unhappy now seem so joyful, when my nephews would get their hands so filthy playing with dirt that when we'd return to my sister's house, instead of taking a bath or going to the movies, I'd have to clean their nails with Carpincho saddle soap as if they'd been down at police headquarters leaving fateful fingerprints.

Though I've always thought it useless to write a book, I now find it is something I must do in order to keep a sacred promise.

Three months ago, I boarded the Anacreonte bound for Capetown, to visit the less tedious side of my family: a consul and his wife, cousins who always looked out for me. Everything we want too much turns out badly or never happens at all. I got sick and had to return as soon as I arrived, because of an accident I had during the trip over there. I fell into the ocean. I slipped on the deck where they store the lifeboats when I leaned over the handrail to reach for a brooch that had fallen off and was dangling from my scarf. How? I don't know. Nobody saw me fall. Maybe I fainted. I came to in the water, dazed by the blow. I couldn't even remember my name. The ship was calmly moving away. I shouted. Nobody heard me. The ship seemed more immense than the sea. Fortunately, I'm a strong swimmer, though my form is quite deficient. After the first shock of cold and fear had passed, I glided slowly through the water. The heat, the noonday light helped me along. I almost forgot my fearful predicament because I love sports, and I tried out all the styles of strokes. At the same time, I thought of the dangers the water could inflict upon me: sharks, sea serpents, jellyfish, waterspouts. The ebb and flow of the waves calmed me down. I swam or floated on my back for eight straight hours, waiting for the ship to return to pick me up. I sometimes wonder how I managed to nurture that hope: I honestly don't know. At first, I felt so much fear that I couldn't think, then thoughts entered my mind haphazardly: I thought of schoolteachers, noodles, movies, prices, theater productions, the names of writers, titles of books, buildings, gardens, a cat, an unhappy love affair, a chair, a flower whose name I couldn't remember, a perfume, a brand of toothpaste, and so on. Memory: how you made me suffer! I suspected that I was about to die or that I had already died in the confusion of my memories. Then I noticed, feeling a sharp burning in my eyes from the saltwater, that

I was alive and far from dying, since those who are drowning are happy, as everyone knows, but I was not. After undressing, or rather, being undressed by the sea in that way the sea undresses a person, with the hands of a lover, there came a moment when sleep or the craving for sleep took hold of me. In order not to sleep, I imposed an order on my thoughts, a kind of mental journey or itinerary I now recommend to prisoners or patients who cannot move or to those desperate souls on the verge of suicide.

I began my itinerary of memories with names and even biographical descriptions, down to the last detail, of people I had known in my life. Naturally, they didn't emerge from my memory in chronological order or in the pecking order of my feelings for them, but instead appeared in a capricious way—the last were the first, and the first were the last, as if my mind couldn't obey the dictates of my heart. In my memory, some people appeared without a name, others were ageless, others from a time when I didn't know them, others without the certainty that they were real people and not ghosts or inventions of my imagination. I didn't recall the eyes of some of them, the hands of others, and in the case of others their hair, their height, their voice. In a way, like Scheherazade to King Shahryar, I told stories to death so that it would spare my life and my images, stories that seemed to never end. I often laugh thinking of that illusory order I invented that seemed so severe when I put it into practice. Sometimes I was surprised by the vivid presence of what I was imagining, formulated in a single phrase, like a vignette inserted at the end of a chapter or introducing the book's most important pages. Naturally, the order is respected in a different way when it's only in the mind rather than written down on the page. As far as possible, I will try to reconstruct in these pages the order or disorder that I constructed with such difficulty in my mind, from the moment in which I glimpsed in the water, as if through a glass window, a sea turtle resembling the tailor Aldo Bindo, which made me recall, through a whimsical association of ideas, Marina Dongui (behind the window of a fruit store), who, like him, had a beauty mark on her left cheek. I began to enumerate and to describe people:

MARINA DONGUI

Marina Dongui, the fruit seller, was the first to appear involuntarily before me in my memory. Blond, fair-skinned and jittery, she would come to the door of the fruit shop whenever I was passing by with my brother, to wink at him. Her breasts were like large fruits overflowing her décolleté, and my brother would pause to look at her—but what am I saying?—not at her but at her breasts, and not at the navel oranges, which were very expensive.

"Miss Marina, how much are the oranges?" my brother would ask.

"The price is right here," she'd say, indicating the label with a plump hand and, picking up an orange, she'd display it with a caress and an indecent smile certainly meant to provoke my brother, who's a handsome lout.

Beneath her blue skirt you could make out the mark on her thighs where her girdle squeezed too tightly. The skin on her bare legs was very smooth and white, turning to a splotchy red damask down near her shoes, which were always black, with spiked heels.

"Miss Marina, give me half a dozen oranges."

"Why oranges, when they're our least favorite fruit?"
I'd protest, feeling the sting of jealousy that pitiful Marina
provoked in me.

*The humiliation of jealousy is not being able to choose the object that
arouses it.*

My brother Mingo would approach the counter without listening to me and there, a vein protruding on his
forehead that appeared only when he was worked up, he'd
corner her against the crates while she was tallying the
total on the piece of paper she'd then use to wrap the oranges, taking advantage of the occasion to feel her up.
It was a fruit relationship, perhaps symbolizing sex. But
I'm getting away from the task I've set myself, that is, to
describe people and not situations or relationships.

I've forgotten my brother's face; I can't even remember the color of his eyes, striped blue and green like glass
marbles.

Sometimes too much love makes it difficult to remember.

But whom did I love?

ALDO BINDO

Aldo Bindo was short, fat, and pale, and spent his
Sundays horseback riding. His glasses shone on his face
like a shop window; he had two tufts of hair on his elongated head, one curly and blond and the other straight
and white. He was ageless. With a measuring tape draped
like a shawl around his shoulders, he would run out of
the back room of the shop when told that I was waiting for him. I'd already have put on the tailored suit,
and, kneeling at my feet, he'd look at me in the mirror,

covered in pins. Often he'd take my measurements all over again as if he didn't already know them. With a pencil that was down to the size of a fingernail, he noted the measurements on a piece of brown wrapping paper he always had at the ready on some chair. As he took my chest measurements, he would touch with satisfaction certain protuberances on the lapel that were both expertly and indecently placed, such details being pertinent to his profession. When he measured my hips, he'd impatiently loop the tape measure around them and then let it fall as if disappointed, releasing one end and catching it with the other hand, and then wind the tape around his neck again. His wife, beside the mirror, her soft white face like a shapeless loaf of bread, passed him the pins and chalk. Sometimes she'd be taking a seam apart with enormous scissors so that he, like a master chef with a ball of dough, could skillfully take up the pieces of cloth and pin them back together to adjust a pleat without actually improving it. He would furrow his brow and, when he had a cold, he sneezed with a sound that was contagious, even over the telephone. His hands seemed to prefer placing sleeves, lapels, and buttons on the bust of a jacket, anything near the breasts of his clients—provided they weren't too elderly. He'd wheeze. He'd pant: the hem tormented him. Just applying some lines with chalk was not enough to release him from his responsibility; he used the tape to measure the hem all the way down to the floor. The shoes he wore always creaked. It never occurred to me that he had feet with toenails or with toes stuck inside those impenetrable shoes. One day I ran into him on the beach and didn't recognize him from a distance, but when he adjusted his wife's beach wrap about her shoulders, I shouted, "There's Aldo Bindo!" and ran over to greet him. Smeared with suntan oil, his face shone with happiness, but where was his measuring tape? He could do nothing without his measuring tape, right? A few minutes later, as he spoke admiringly of Mrs. Cerunda, I saw that he was using his big toe to sketch a measuring tape in the damp sand.

In those days I fell in love with the sea as though it were a person. At vacation's end, before returning to Buenos Aires, I would kneel down crying, to bid it farewell.

ALINA CERUNDA

Alina Cerunda was pretty despite her seventy years. Anyone who says she wasn't is a liar. However, old people always look like they're in disguise, and that ruins everything. I have it on good authority that she never bathed. But she looked clean, with impeccably coiffed hair, styled in a pouf even when she slept. I've seen Alina Cerunda in bed, like a painting. Surrounded by small balls of yarn of various colors, as if in an unsavory nest, she knitted darling little dressing gowns for newborns, or booties with pom-poms for the ill or the elderly. Often I would watch her, a veritable guardian angel of nutrition, as she made crème brûlée and flan, ladyfingers and *alfajores*. Tall and thin, with white and blue hair like birthday cake trimmings, I consider her among the most beautiful of women. Sometimes her eyelids can become red with fatigue; on her, weariness is a pigment that makes her eyes larger. If she were my mother I'd have her portrait done by a skilled painter and hang it in the most conspicuous place in the house. What a family keepsake! Her green eyes matched the color of her collar, which was also green.

But why do I remember so many things that do me no good? How tedious it was to be with Alina Cerunda! And why am I thinking about her now? Could it be a bad omen?

GABRIELA

Just like that time when I was sick, and after being in bed for forty days I missed my bed, now I miss the sea. Ah, the sea. "The sea full of masculine urgency." Whose line was that? Gabriela, oh how beautiful she was! Her eyes were the color of the sea.

In a mosaic inside the Basilica of Saint Apollinaris, in Ravenna, the archangel Gabriel has big astonished eyes, gently curling hair parted down the middle, a small and slender nose, a well-defined mouth with the corner of the lips turning downward on the right side, a mild expression and a saintly halo over a rounded and not very long oval face, a white tunic and two large wings. Poor Irene had clipped the photograph of that mosaic from a magazine, first to jot down an address on the other side of the page, then, because she liked it, she kept it under glass for eight years in her single room. She used to say that she had looked at that image absent-mindedly many times during her pregnancy, never thinking that her daughter would look so much like him. She was frequently surprised that Gabriela wasn't a boy, didn't have wings or a strange frock like the one in the image. It became her habit to call her Gabriel, to shorten the name a bit and because she liked saying Gabriel better than

Gabriela. She recalled the years of her own childhood in Spain, so different from Gabriel's. That she'd been born in Spain seemed like a dream to her. She wasn't aware of the feeling of neglect that she sometimes inflicted on her daughter, and believed that she herself had been the most neglected girl in the world. She was three or four years old when her mother remarried, to a man who didn't want to endure the presence of someone else's children. They lived in Ginzo de Limia, a poor and isolated village. In less than nine months, her mother abandoned Irene and her sister, who was older. They begged in the street. They were given shelter in the attic of a brothel and received the leftover food at the end of each day.

It was sometime later, when she found out those women were prostitutes, that she appreciated the kindness (it had seemed natural to her then) that they had shown her and her sister. She vividly remembered a particular woman who would always step out on the balcony to take the fresh air, even in winter when snow was falling. She held Irene in her arms when she cried, like a mother would. When Irene had to leave that house (which she had begun to feel was her home) because her repentant stepfather had sent for them, she cried for that woman as she'd never cried for anyone. The time she spent in her stepfather's house before sailing for Argentina was brief. One day, the most memorable, her drunken stepfather tied a rope around her waist and swung her from the first-floor balcony until a crowd of villagers gathered, none of them daring to say a thing for fear that the man would drop her. Entertained by the game, she hadn't realized the danger she'd been in.

Everything else was erased from her memory and came back as memories of baby teeth, the first day of school, Buenos Aires, the different people, the flat landscape, the river everywhere, the difficulties of life in the home of the aunt who had taken her in, the changes of childhood, her clothing becoming too small, life's many lessons (how to wash your face, brush your teeth, get dressed, eat, urinate and defecate correctly), adolescence, coming of age. Upon discovering love, she believed in its fleeting salvation. News of the death of her mother (a death that was never explained), who had lain for twelve hours in the snowy woods and, by some miracle, had not been devoured by wolves, tormented her. As if that weren't enough, sometime later, her husband abandoned her to run off with another woman, and then there was Gabriel, Gabriel, Gabriel and Leandro . . . but Gabriel most of all.

I glimpsed a flash of lightning in the sky, then another and yet another. If I were brave, how I would have loved to see a storm let loose. I closed my eyes. It rained a little. I opened my eyes again. The clouds were going away. Why won't they take me with them!

IRENE ROCA

Irene was not at all like her daughter. Irene had a joyful nature. Her even features made one think of a faded porcelain doll. Gabriela was waiting for Irene in Plaza Las Heras. She had followed her that day, which I'm remembering now as Irene's face comes back to me. She was so pretty dressed in green with that necklace of tiny pearls, and a pair of white gloves she carried in her hand like a bouquet! Gabriela lost sight of her in a moment of distraction, in front of a tobacco shop where they sold marbles. I saw her sitting pitifully on a green wooden bench eating an orange and staring, without realizing it, at the door her mother had entered.

What do women do when they're not at home? When they were pure like her mother they devoted themselves to serious tasks, Gabriela might think. Then she'd think, as usual, about the sex act. What she desired most in the universe of her curiosity was to see a man and a woman doing it. She had seen cats, dogs, pigeons, *guanacos*, monkeys commit that act, but never human beings. Juancha, a schoolmate, had told her that it was lots of fun.

To make her way to that disorderly room, with books on the floor, socks over the chairs, half-open sacks of bread on a table, shirts tossed on the floor, Irene had crossed a vestibule with an interior door whose glass panes were red and blue, blue like the color of the ocean I'm looking at, then a courtyard with plants, birdcages and a lemon tree in the center. I knew that room. But how different was the place Gabriela imagined her in, engaged in mysterious occupations!

What was her mother doing? She thought of nothing else. Irene had told her that in the house she was visiting there was a mechanical bird that sang inside a glass cage with gold trim. Liar. How she lied to her. That glass and gold cage occupied a predominant place in Gabriela's imagination. It had turned into a palace illuminated by a thousand chandeliers, a palace where her mother wove beautiful cloth with her perfumed and kindhearted friends.

She crossed many rooms and gardens before reaching the place where he was waiting for her. There, in a kind of cloister, was an enormous fishbowl with fish covered in purple fins and tails. This was Valentín Masini's dry cleaners, where they never took Gabriela because the fumes of ammonium and other acids were not good for her health.

The sun lit up the mirror of a wardrobe with the face of a faun, bunches of grapes, and leaves sculpted into the wood; a tiger-striped cat slept on a simple bed with a peeling iron frame, while torn, dirty curtains waved in the breeze. I liked that room! Irene did too. Sitting on the floor, her elbow leaning on the bed, she would occasionally glance at the disorder, as if it bothered her, then return again to the book she was reading. Sometimes one of her brassieres or handkerchiefs would be left on the floor. I looked at them with such hatred the first time I found them, without knowing to whom they belonged. She, Irene, was part of that disorder, one of its makers and also one of its martyrs. Stretching like an idiot, she'd call out to Leandro in a shrill voice. Did she love him? Was that what love looked like?

Often I imagined this scene that tortured me so. He had told me about it. Not even the sea makes me forget it.

Leandro's muffled voice, from under the shower, would respond as usual:

"What do you want?"

He'd tell me in detail the silly things they'd say.

"I can't be a minute without you, my love," she'd always say to him.

"I'm coming," he'd answer, annoyed.

"Could you explain that matter of the synapses of the

nervous system or about the extra-systolic pathways of the respiratory system?

"It would be better if they didn't exist," Leandro would reply, drying his face with a towel; none of it mattered to him, and he would add vehemently: "It would be better if humanity didn't exist, human beings are utter crap." As he entered the room his body gleamed like the body of the bronze statue in the museum that Irene had sketched in her adolescence. How well I could imagine him! He always seemed happy.

"Don't ask me to explain anything to you today. I have to go to the hospital. I don't have time for anything. I've got to leave right now."

"So early? Who are you going to see?"

"Nobody. Don't pester me with questions. I have to feel free, don't you understand? I can't be tied down," Leandro would answer as he dressed.

Sometimes when I have a fever I hear this conversation, with their voices buzzing like bees. How salty the sea is!

"Idiot," Irene would say. She was the idiot and she knew it. She'd think *that "nobody" is worse than if it were somebody.*

Nino, purring, would come over and rub against Leandro's legs. He was a dreadful cat, with his face split by a black stripe, which Gabriela would have liked because he looked like a tiger, and he adored me.

"Not tied down," Irene would continue, "as if you could live without ties. You even carry on a relationship with that ridiculous cat. You never go to bed without saying 'Good night, Mr. Cat,' as if you were a little boy. This rug is full of fleas."

As he did with me, Leandro paid her no attention,

whistling as he looked at himself in the mirror. Irene's words seemed ridiculous to him, and her attitude unpleasant. Pathetically, Irene would suddenly go over to hug him. The sensual voice has meaning beyond the words uttered, but she seemed so disagreeably human to him, there in the mirror.

"Won't you explain about nerve synapses or the urinary tract? If you don't explain it, I'll never understand, not with the help of pictures or textbooks or even with hands-on practice," she'd say to him every day, playing the doctor. It was always the same, always the same.

"Irene, don't you think we're letting life slip through our fingers studying together like this? You'll never understand that there's not enough time to go sneaking around."

"Let's not start that eternal argument again. You've changed in the last two months, ever since you've been living here. I want to graduate, I want to have a profession. I want to study. I'm doing it for Gabriela. She's the only person who loves me. The only one!"

"Which do you prefer: to love or to be loved?" Leandro interrupted her.

He'd say the same to me, but I'd just smile.

"To love," Irene would answer.

"Love me, then."

Lying on the bed, Irene would embrace Leandro once again. He would kiss her passionately, the way he kissed me. The same thing would happen whenever she mentioned Gabriela. Leandro needed Irene to love another being that wasn't him in order to feel any interest in her. It is so overwhelming to be loved exclusively.

"Does she always follow you?"

"She's probably on the corner. I don't dare to go out," Irene would remark. "She's so young, but she understands so many things! She's not like other little girls. Look at her, isn't she lovely?"

Leandro would adjust his tie and finish dressing, looking out the window at the girl on the street.

"Lovely," he'd say, thinking of something else.

For him, children weren't as marvelous as they were for me, they were a concoction smelling of milk and oranges, they were creatures from another planet—especially that Gabriela, or Gabriel, whose name, constantly changing back and forth from feminine to masculine like a hermaphrodite, was always on Irene's lips.

"Poor Gabriel," Irene would murmur, "sometimes I feel guilty."

"About what?"

"About everything," Irene would answer.

"Don't forget to lock the door and leave the key in the big planter in the courtyard. I have to go."

That was how it was, every day always the same, always the same.

"You're not even going to give me a kiss?" Irene would sigh.

"Didn't I kiss you enough?"

"Each of your kisses is a dream. Nothing seems real. It's as if I'm embracing you at the bottom of the sea and cease to exist. Later, when I'm alone, I still don't exist, but then it's unpleasant."

Uttering this sentence, Irene would feel that she had destroyed the importance of her feelings, and she had. Why explain them? Bitterly, she would hear Leandro's voice.

"You're always so sentimental. What a pity!"

After kissing Irene again impatiently, mussing her hair, hurting her lips, Leandro would pick up the books that lay on the table.

These unpleasant scenes repeat over and over again. He's going to hate me, Irene would think. *When a man doesn't love you, his embraces become awkward. He has too many arms and legs, too many bones, elbows and knees. It's almost impossible for him to produce an orgasm. He used to slide over me like water, now he hurts me.*

She was right. Poor Irene, I alone understood her. Alone, alone as I am now, on a sea of relentless doubts. Dying is the only sure thing. Now I can finally die. But how to do it? It's as impossible as ever.

GABRIELA

Gabriela. I return to Gabriela. She was lovely, with a long slender neck, blue eyes, blond hair. I always said she could be in the movies; what she needed were connections; you don't get anywhere these days without connections. She lived for Irene.

Alone, she would wait for Irene, always in Plaza Las Heras. She had followed her that day, which I remember now, more vividly than other days. She was so pretty, dressed in green with that necklace of tiny pearls, and a pair of white gloves she carried in her hand like a bouquet! Gabriela lost sight of her in a moment of distraction, in front of a tobacco shop where they sold marbles. She sat pitifully on a green wooden bench eating an orange and staring, without realizing it, at the door her mother had entered.

What do women do when they're not at home? When

they were pure like her mother they would be devoting themselves to serious tasks, she might think. Then she'd no doubt think, as usual, about the sex act. What she desired most in the universe of her curiosity was to see a man and a woman doing it. She had seen cats, dogs, pigeons, *guanacos*, monkeys commit that act, but never human beings. Juancha, a schoolmate, had told her that it was lots of fun. Juancha was a slut.

I knew that to make her way to that disorderly room, with books on the floor, socks over the chairs, half-opened sacks of bread on a table, shirts tossed on the floor, Irene had crossed a vestibule with an interior door whose glass panes were red and blue; then a courtyard with plants, birdcages and a lemon tree in the center. But how different was the place Gabriela imagined her in, engaged in mysterious occupations! What was her mother doing? Irene had told her that in the house she was visiting there was a mechanical bird that sang inside a glass cage with gold trim. That glass and gold cage occupied a predominant place in Gabriela's imagination. It had turned into a palace illuminated by a thousand chandeliers, a palace where her mother wove beautiful cloth with her perfumed and kind-hearted friends. She crossed many rooms and gardens before reaching the place where he waited for her. There, in a kind of cloister, was an enormous fishbowl with fish covered in purple fins and tails. This was Valentín Masini's dry cleaners, where they never took Gabriela because the fumes of ammonium and other acids were not good for her health.

The sun lit up the mirror of a wardrobe with the face of a faun, bunches of grapes, and leaves sculpted into the wood; a tiger-striped cat slept on a simple bed with a peeling iron frame, while torn dirty curtains waved in the breeze. Irene, sitting on the floor, her elbow leaning on the bed, would occasionally glance at the disorder as if it bothered her, then return again to the book she was reading. She, Irene, was part of that disorder, one of its makers and also one of its martyrs. Stretching, she called out to Leandro in a shrill voice. Did she love him?

Leandro's muffled voice, from under the shower, responded as usual:

"What do you want?"

"I can't be a minute without you, my love."

"I'm coming."

"Could you explain that matter of the sensitive respiratory passages?"

"It would be better if they didn't exist," Leandro replied, drying his face with a towel, adding vehemently: "It would be better if humanity didn't exist, to suffer so much." As he entered the room his body gleamed like the body of the bronze statue in the museum that Irene had sketched in her adolescence. He seemed happy.

"Don't ask me to explain anything to you today. I have to go to the hospital. I don't have time for anything. I've got to leave right now."

"So early? Who are you going to see?"

"Nobody. Don't pester me with questions. I have to feel free, don't you understand? I can't be tied down, " Leandro answered as he dressed.

"Idiot," said Irene. And she thought *that "nobody" is worse than if it were somebody.*

She was right.

The cat, purring, came over and rubbed against Leandro's legs.

He was a dreadful cat, with his face split by a black stripe, which Gabriela would have liked because he looked like a tiger.

"Not tied down," Irene continued, "as if you could live without ties. You even carry on a relationship with that ridiculous cat. You never go to bed without saying, 'Good night, Mr. Cat,' as if you were a little boy. This rug is full of fleas."

Leandro paid no attention, whistling as he looked at himself in the mirror. Irene's words seemed ridiculous to him, and her attitude unpleasant. Irene suddenly went over to hug him. The sensual voice has meaning beyond the words uttered, but she seemed so disagreeably human to him, there in the mirror.

"Won't you explain about nerve synapses or the urinary tract? If you don't explain it, I'll never understand, not with the help of pictures or textbooks or even with hands-on practice."

"Irene, don't you think we're letting life slip through our fingers studying together like this? You'll never understand that there's not enough time to go sneaking around."

"Let's not start that eternal argument again. You've changed in the last two months, ever since you've been living here. I want to graduate, I want to have a profession. I want to study. I'm doing it for Gabriel. She's the only person who loves me. The only one!"

"Which do you prefer: to love or to be loved?" Leandro interrupted her.

"To love," Irene answered.

"Love me, then."

Lying on the bed, Irene embraced Leandro once again. He kissed her passionately. The same thing happened whenever she mentioned Gabriel. Leandro needed Irene to love another being that wasn't him in order to feel any interest in her. It is so overwhelming to be loved exclusively.

"Does she always follow you?"

"She's probably on the corner. I don't dare to go out," Irene remarked. "She's so young, but she understands so many things! She's not like other little girls. Look at her, isn't she lovely?"

Leandro adjusted his tie and finished dressing, looking out the window at the girl on the street.

"Lovely," he said. For him, children weren't as marvelous as they were for me, they were a concoction smelling of milk and oranges, they were creatures from another planet—especially that Gabriela, whose name, constantly changing back and forth from feminine to masculine, was always on Irene's lips.

"Poor Gabriela," Irene murmured, "sometimes I feel guilty."

"About what?"

"About everything," Irene answered.

"Don't forget to lock the door and leave the key in the big planter in the courtyard. I have to go."

"You're not even going to give me a kiss?" Irene sighed.

"Didn't I kiss you enough?"

"Each of your kisses is a dream. Nothing seems real.

It's as if I'm embracing you at the bottom of the sea and cease to exist. Later, when I'm alone, I still don't exist, but then it's unpleasant."

Uttering this sentence, Irene felt that she had destroyed the importance of her feelings, and she had. Why explain them? Bitterly, she heard Leandro's voice.

"You're always so sentimental. What a pity!"

After kissing Irene again impatiently, mussing her hair, hurting her lips, Leandro picked up two books that lay on the table and a magazine where I saw the photograph of Mr. Pigmy that same evening.

Can one make love in the sea? So often I tried to commit suicide, and now that I could do it easily, I can't.

MR. PIGMY

I know Mr. Pigmy from photographs, but in this moment his face is as familiar as that of any friend. An uncle of mine once showed him to me among photos of the Congo, which had appeared in a magazine. While I was looking at the colossal and mischievous face of the dwarf, he told me the story of the explorer Mattheus who had taken him out of the benevolent and innocent jungle. As soon as Mr. Pigmy found himself outside the jungle he no longer recognized the world. He believed that three zebras he glimpsed in the distance were three very strange animals two centimeters tall. He believed that a tree was a tuft of grass, that a man was an ant; he didn't understand the laws of perspective. Not long after his exile, Mr. Pigmy died of sadness. In a way he had been killed by the sun, since during his twenty-five years of life in the jungle, the sun's rays had always been gently filtered by the damp protective leaves of the tropical trees. In the summer, I've slept under their cool and perfumed blanket. This is why I remember so precisely that black shiny face, that body, small and potbellied as if it belonged to my family, to a member of my family who could have gone away on a trip before I was born, never to return. His slightly bulging round eyes, pointy chin, and flat nose seemed incapable of expressing the sadness of his soul. I still feel as sorry for him as when I first heard his story. I was in bed with a fever. I suspected that my uncle had fallen in love with me, or I with him, because sick people disgusted him, and I didn't. He drank from my glass looking at Mr. Pigmy's face.

"Being tired is restful, while resting is not always restful," Leandro used to say. He was right. The same water that kills now revives me.

LEANDRO ÁLVAREZ

Leandro Álvarez's face was as changeable as the weather. His eyes could be gray, green, and even blue. I don't want to think about him. He was too young for my taste and talked to me as if I were his conscience. Everything he told me now feels like it happened to me. I want to think of other people, but I always come back to Leandro.

Leandro opened the door, slammed it closed again, and went out to the courtyard filled with plants and canaries. He was tired of Irene, but he loved her, and that was the worst. The worst is never letting go completely of love. He was bored with her, as he was with his own conscience. The spring sun on the wisteria accented the blue color of the sky. The leaves cast shadows shaped like spiders and hands onto the flagstone. The owner of the

boardinghouse, in her gray-striped apron, was watering
the plants. The smell of hot, wet soil, the smell of the
countryside in that enclosure under the sky, reminded
him of his childhood, as it did me. Outside on the street,
a group of children were fighting over a box in which they
were dragging a dead cat. Leandro thought: *I should say
something to them. The cat is rotting. But they might throw stones at me.*
(He was a coward, but that didn't matter to me.) A knife
grinder passed by with his cart, hawking his services with
a whistle. Leandro marveled at the day. He stopped before reaching the corner. He glimpsed the nearby store,
Circe Antiquities, always with its lit chandeliers and a
double bed that had not been put together yet. He tied
his shoelace. He found it all so depressing. How he made
me suffer!

I'm not going to have any luck, he always thought. One day,
he noticed he was stepping on some sheets of handwritten
pages folded in fourths. He picked up the pages, unfolded
them, and looked around to see where they'd come from.
He was a little embarrassed to see that a street cleaner was
watching him. In the window of an upper-story apartment, a young woman quickly peered out; he wasn't able
to see her clearly. The kids, dragging the box, passed by.
Leandro looked up again. Many windows were open, and
one could glimpse the curtains, bedcovers, sheets and
closets. Something indecently intimate emanated from
the houses, odors that one could divine. He put the pages
in his pocket and kept walking. He took out a cigarette.
On the corner, the same girl, poorly dressed, was leaning
against the wall.

That's Gabriel, Irene's daughter, Leandro thought: *she doesn't look like her mother. She's almost always dressed like a man because, as Irene explained to me, men's clothing is cheaper and it keeps her from getting her legs dirty.* He looked at her sideways and kept on walking. "Poor Gabriel," he remembered Irene always lamenting. Irene was bourgeois. There's always something in the dramatic life of a woman that makes her bourgeois. I agreed with him. In front of a barbershop, Leandro saw a man smoking and asked him for a light. While he lit his cigarette, he looked at the man's beard and eyeglasses, the patches on his suit, the cuffs of his shirt, *dirty like mine,* he thought, *I should wear short sleeves.* He walked along the tree-lined streets, went into the botanical garden, past the shadows of the palm trees and the greenhouses. Under the foliage he remembered a beach: the air undressed him. He sat on a marble bench, then lay down face up to the sun and looked past the cigarette smoke at the statue of Pliny. He took out the slim folded packet again, read the pages attentively.

A woman with loose long hair, wandering in the garden while licking an ice cream cone, observed him from a distance. She came over and leaned her knees against Leandro's legs. Wiggling her body she finished the ice cream, making noises with her tongue. Leandro didn't interrupt his reading. A flower the woman wore in her hair fell on his head, and Leandro finally looked at her. *She's a prostitute,* he thought, *they've never interested me, not even in the best places.* He caught a whiff of her hair that emanated a dirty brush smell in the heat, like the heads of those people in his childhood kneeling in confessionals, smelling of cheap perfume and powders, of barbershop pomade. Leandro managed to make this memory mine.

"You need a bath," he said to scare her away.

She, thinking he was flirting, looked down at him shaking her red mane.

"Did the garbage truck come through here?" Leandro said in an obscene tone. Who was he imitating, some poseur from the university? It was the kind of thing a friend of his would have said in a similar situation.

"Shithead!" she snapped back, stamping the ground and raising a cloud of dust with her heels. "You worthless bum!" she shouted as Leandro vanished through the trees, and she headed for the greenhouses.

An effeminate young man in a blue blouse, with a book under his arm, looked at him persistently. Everyone fell in love with him. A vague odor of sweat and cosmetics poisoned the air. Five old men were arguing on a bench. He consulted his watch: time to go to the hospital. How quickly time passed when he wasn't doing anything. Everyone fell in love with him, even Zulma.

And if right now a whale appeared, or a swordfish or a sea lion, what would I do? At least the sea doesn't have those amphibians I find so disgusting. How far I must be from the coast, as far away as my salvation!

ZULMA

Zulma lived next door when I was a child. Older than me, she'd made friends with my sisters. She had pale golden skin and light-brown hair, like the color of her eyes. Slender and agile, she would peer out the front door of her house, always hiding as if spying. Skinny as she was, she had thick, muscular legs. She was a ballerina. Every day we'd hear the piano that accompanied the exercises she did in the inner courtyard of her house. When the door was ajar, the people who walked by would stop to watch her, and the boys always said something obscene or paid her compliments. Almost naked in the summertime, or in a heavy leotard in the winter, she'd continue doing her exercises without paying attention to the comments from her fans or curious passers-by. After a while, Zulma had students and a big mirror in the dining room, which allowed her and her students to observe the rhythmic movements of the dance they were rehearsing. Her godmother, who was obese, would drink wine as she watched her dance. The piano chords were so out of tune that it seemed they'd traveled through water or outer space. I don't know the pianist, who I probably never met and who had flaming red hair and bit her nails. I went into Zulma's house twice or maybe three times, tagging along with my sisters who'd gone over for a visit. The obese godmother, light as a balloon, would be in the corner drinking red wine. For hours I watched Zulma do the exercises that she called "rhythmics," exercises that made her look like a wounded bird trying to fly. I found out that Zulma had once fallen in love with a young man, who left her. But this did not cause her to give up her devotion to ballet. She was a real ballerina and should have danced in the Colon Theater.

The time came when I would no longer see her peer out the door of her house, nor hear the piano. The godmother was no longer seen drinking in a corner. I asked after Zulma. They told me that so much exercising made her body lose the weight needed to stay rooted on earth. She always looked as if she were about to fly away, and she had, just as the pigeons in the courtyard had flown away when the house was torn down months after her disappearance.

"And the fat godmother?" I asked.

"She flew away too. Haven't you seen how balloons fly?" they answered me. "Ask Susana."

What exists at the bottom of this ocean? Shipwrecked vessels? Debris? The sea eats up everything. One day, any second now, it will eat me up too.

SUSANA

The first I see of Susana are her dark, shiny eyes, then the sad, smiling mouth, then hands that explain what her words tell. She shivers with the fear she feels about premonitions: a black spider on her bed, in winter, in her house, in the city.

A young Peruvian medical student rushes over when she calls, to give a shot of penicillin to her sister. It's three o'clock in the morning. Susana is nervous while he sterilizes the syringe and the needle with boiling water.

The Peruvian asks her:

"Aren't you tired? Have you slept?"

Susana answers:

"No, I can't sleep."

"Do you like peaches in syrup?" the Peruvian asks.

"Yes," answers Susana, who has a sweet tooth. "Why?"

"Well, eat two or three peaches, they will have a soothing effect on the mucous membranes, they're calming," said the Peruvian.

When the Peruvian returns at seven in the evening, Susana yawns.

"Are you sleepy?" he asks her.

"Very," Susana answers. "I'm so tired."

"Do you like peaches in syrup?"

"Very much. Why?"

"Have two or three slices. They're great for the mucous membranes. They revitalize your energy."

The next day when the Peruvian returns, Susana's sister complains of a slight pain in the stomach.

"Does she like peaches in syrup? They relieve pain."

"You've really got a thing about peaches in syrup!" Susana exclaims.

"Do you like them a lot?" asks Susana's sister.

The Peruvian puckers his lips (I knew the Peruvian) as if he were about to kiss those imaginary peaches.

"I'm crazy about them."

That night at eight o'clock Susana buys a can of peaches in syrup, eats them with her sister and regrets not sharing them with the Peruvian.

As for me, I like fresh peaches—like the peaches Aldo used to give me!

That yellowing photo of Aldo I kept in my pocketbook and that traveled with me when we'd go out to the countryside, never faded. I would take it with me to the bottom of the sea so that nobody could steal it from me.

ALDO FABRICI

Fabrici, stooped over, with his arms akimbo on each side of his body as if he were carrying watering cans, pails, or garden tools, was a very old gardener. I was very fond of him because, when I was a child, he gave me fruit, nuts, lettuce for my dolls. His big eyes always looked surprised,

and when words failed him, he managed to express himself with his long hands that were like tentacles, enormous sweet potatoes or monstrous roots. Clean, orderly,
devout, he'd place flowers in a glass in front of a print
of the Virgin in the tool shed. Aldo gathered the oranges and lemons, the walnuts and chestnuts, the peaches,
to distribute them. He never missed Mass on Sundays.
He had a twenty-year-old girlfriend, and he brought her
fruit and a bunch of flowers every week. Why are people named after flowers and not fruits? There is nobody
named Strawberry or Raspberry or Apricot, which are
lovelier than Lily.

What is falling in love, anyway? Letting go of disgust,
of fear, letting go of everything.

Flying fish remind me of butterflies in flight.

What is magical about the sea is that living deep inside
it no one can speak.

LILY AND LILLIAN

Lily and Lillian were always together. Everyone thought
they were sisters because they wore the same color. Lily
was blond and Lillian dark-haired, but sometimes
Lillian dyed her hair blond and looked even more like
Lily. People who love each other end up seeming identi-
cal, saying the same words, moving their hands with the
same gestures, and biting their lips in the same way. At
the age of twenty they fell in love—or believed they fell in
love—with the same man. One would see the boy in the
morning, and the other in the afternoon. He thought he
was deceiving them both, but he wasn't deceiving anyone.
The two of them were deceiving him, because instead of

kissing him they were kissing each other, instead of adoring him they adored one another.

How green the sea was! How green and how blue! I would like to swim for hours and hours. But aren't I in the sea now?

LEANDRO

Again I'm thinking about Leandro, again I mention him because that day Leandro was another man, his eyes were green, he'd grown a beard, and he seemed dirty, filthy dirty. What a pity! He was moving his chin like a ruminant, but what struck me were the secrets he revealed.

Every time Leandro went out he would inspect the neighboring houses in hopes of seeing the girl he'd glimpsed on the balcony the day he found the pages. He admitted this to me reluctantly. With summer approaching, the streets were busier, and the chance of coming across the woman to whom the pages belonged would be even more difficult. Nevertheless, he did not give up on the hope he had when he first found the pages, his hope for an affair. In that text, so fragmentary, a name stood out as already familiar to him. That awful name invited him to read and reread.

Long summers without vacations horrified Leandro. Irene was already boring him like a sister or like me. Seeing her all the time made time go slower. He had to invent something new in his life, something that had to be completely absurd: a bundle of pages written by an unknown hand. One evening, coming home in a taxi with me, as he was paying, he saw the pages he'd picked up a few days earlier on the street in his wallet, folded in such a way that the word LEA, as if commanding him to read, stood out among the others. And just then, at the entrance to the apartment building next to his, he saw a hearse with the same letters. The letters stood out against the black cloth. The crowd gathered at the door looked appreciatively at the parade of floral wreathes and sprays and people in mourning. In the crowd he saw or he thought he saw Gabriela. "That girl is everywhere," he said to me. Leandro had a heart of stone. He went into the crowd and questioned a woman wearing a ridiculous hat.

"Who died?"

"Leonor. Don't you know her? But yes: Leonor Eladia Arévalo. They called her Lea because her initials formed that name."

There are ridiculous names that affect us deeply, names with faces, with hands, with a voice! Why did he tell me that!

Determined, Leandro made his way through the flowers and the people, pushing into the house where there was a wake being held for the deceased. I followed him like a shadow. We stepped into the dark elevator with the lady wearing that hat that looked like a bird flapping its wings. *People still wear feathers and sequins and wigs*, I thought. "I thought those frills only existed in photos of my great-grandparents. And that perfume that smells like incense, or those black paper fans with jet-black ribs, or those lace gloves that make you clench your teeth when you touch them, they all still exist. How pleasant not to know anyone, to feel like you're in another country, among people who speak another language. To make things less awkward, maybe it's a good idea to pretend that I'm a little deaf," he said to me.

Protected by the gloom and the contact of many hands, Leandro and I entered the wake. The communal hysterics inspired him to be bold. He ceremoniously greeted the women whose heads were bare and eyes were red. A bearded old man embraced him, mistaking him for another young man in the family. A gentleman with a stentorian voice parted the way for him to enter the candlelit chapel.

"You must see her. Her fellow students loved her dearly," said the loud gentleman.

Leandro drew near to the coffin. He thought: *Lea, what a name! Why isn't she called Lia or Luz or Eva? There aren't many names with just three letters in Spanish. A dead woman who's not from my family or to be used for experiments, like in the hospital, looks beautiful to me. At least she can't disappoint me or make me suffer. She's unimaginably breathtaking. Her hair, pale blond, shines like the gold of those antique jewels I like. The color of her skin is neither white nor dark. Perhaps death gives her an ivory tint, or had it been her real coloring? And what if I cut off a lock of her hair? With what? I don't have any scissors. What a pity. If I kissed her on the cheek, what would people think? And what if I gave her a kiss on the lips? Am I capable of doing that? People would think I'd been her lover or that we'd had a romantic friendship.*

Why did he tell me those things: to torment me or to disgust me? Leandro hesitated a moment, then kissed her on the lips: she smelled of paper, of incense, of flowers, of perfume.

Necrophile, how dreadful! I thought. He put his mouth on those hard, marble lips! He liked it! It's monstrous. When you're in love nothing else matters. *They'll throw me* out. *They'll call me a necrophile,* he thought; *I don't care, none of it matters.* He remembered a poor, hungry man who would go to all the wakes just to get something to eat, or an old woman who would steal flowers or teaspoons. Wasn't what he was doing worse? They offered him a cup of coffee to get things back on the right note, perhaps to get him away from the dead woman. He shook his head, raised his eyes and saw that some people were looking at him with compassion, others with horror, or with indignation. He thought: *I could ask the dead woman for something, perhaps I could ask a favor as if she were a saint. But what would I ask for? To come back to life, to be the unknown person I'm looking for, the woman I can never find.*

The man with the booming voice patted him on the shoulder:

"Come say hello to Verónica; they were inseparable, almost twins, born one year apart. She didn't want them to take her away yet." Consulting his wristwatch he added: "The hearse has been waiting outside for some time. They didn't close the coffin. She should be taken out of the room already. They're already taking away the flowers." He took Leandro by the arm and led him over to Verónica, telling her: "He's one of Leonor's fellow students, don't you remember him? No, you didn't know him. You could share your sorrow with him." Then, very ceremoniously, he took Verónica and Leandro to another room where many people were standing around. Three little girls were muffling their laughter in their handkerchiefs; an old woman was crying, praying with her rosary; another was stealthily stealing flowers from the bouquets; one lady was fanning herself with a saint's image.

Verónica and Leandro gave each other a long look, as if studying a postcard; he admitted as much himself.

"Did you know each other for a long time?" Verónica asked, fingering the lapel of her suit that, according to Leandro, was very elegant.

"Quite a while," Leandro answered.

"How similar a wake is to a party. There's the smell of flowers, the eating at all hours and people hugging each other all the time. At parties people hug each other dancing, but at wakes people hug each other crying, that's the only difference. But I can't cry. I envy people who cry; they show off their tears like necklaces. I feel deprived without tears, impoverished, said Verónica, laying it on thick, and moving over to the open shutters. Then, when she saw the sun on Leandro's face, she exclaimed: "How could this be happening on such a nice day!" and, leaning her head against her arm like an actress, she said, "I should have died."

Perhaps Verónica felt laid bare by Leandro's eyes on the back of her neck, just as I felt when I saw him for the first time. Somewhere in her soul perhaps she was in despair over her sister's death, but the lucidity with which she noted every worldly detail around her made her think, in that moment, that her heart was made of ice. Perhaps an inner voice was repeating to her: "I'm a monster, I'm a monster." Leandro thought all this as he looked at the nape of her neck: *"She's pretty. She doesn't look like anyone else, at least."*

"So, do you like her?" he asked me.

I didn't answer him, dropping his clammy hand. He has no soul.

Sonia had the face of a startled fish, faded hair, and a lipless mouth.

Was she miserable? To judge by her laughter she was happy.

The only advantage of being a child is that time is doubly wide, like upholstery fabric. Time, of which there is never enough for anything, was as infinite as a desert for Sonia. Whenever she had a free moment, and these were plentiful, she'd go to the zoo. Like Gabriela, she liked animals because they behaved in a natural way: if they were hungry they ate nonstop, if they were thirsty they drank until they were full, if they were in heat they made love desperately, if they were tired they slept at any hour of the day, if they were furious they bit or scratched or killed their enemy. It is true is that they also died and that dying is ridiculous, but they were so meticulous, so precise. (Sonia would never forget her paternal grandfather's death; an apocryphal death). Sometimes she would give the animals the cookies or chocolates she had been given. Sometimes she would put her hands through the bars to pet them. What could a jaguar, a wolf, a hyena, a tiger do to her? She was the animals' champion. She always brought a little notebook in which, after looking at them for a long while, she would draw them, carefully recording each of their names beneath the drawings, marking her favorites with a star and those she liked least with an x. In her opinion, the ones she liked the least generally resembled certain people. Will I ever think of someone who isn't a person?

Leandro has infinite faces. How to describe one of his faces without destroying the others? This is why I return to him again.

In my mind, Leandro was walking beside me, through endless corridors, hallways, two courtyards; he climbed a flight of stairs and entered a room with me. The interns were smoking and drinking coffee. *This mania for drinking coffee in every common room,* Leandro thought, *why don't they drink something that's better for me?*

That day when he got angry at Mendiondo; their exchange is engraved in my memory.

"Bring me a coffee," he said, annoyed. According to what he told me in endless detail, one of the young interns served him a cup of coffee from a coffeepot sitting over the flame of a heater. Leandro coughed at the first sip: "How disgusting. It tastes like a fly."

"Have you ever eaten flies?" Mendiondo asked.

"Yes, when I was a kid, on a dare. Of course, I tore off the wings and tiny legs before I ate it."

Urbino peered into the room, holding a covered pail. He took the cover off and pulled out a heart, held it under Raco's nose, saying:

"Do you see that he had a lesion in the mitral valve?"

Leandro almost vomited, it was so awful. Waving him away as if waving away an insect, he shouted:

"Get the hell out of here!"

Urbino put his fingers inside the heart. Leandro protested:

"We're eating."

"The top dogs don't like to talk about this," said Urbino, brandishing the heart.

That label, which had so offended Leandro when he first became a doctor, now left him indifferent.

"And the bread, where did you put it?" he asked. "You've all eaten peacefully at home, and here I am starving." From a drawer filled with papers, strings, and other things, Leandro took out a loaf of bread that was already hard. "A fine loaf of bread this is," he exclaimed, "I wonder what dynasty it's from."

"You've always thrived on old relics," Mendiondo answered. "Do you remember the dressmaker's appendix?"

"I'll never forget it. It looked like a leper's penis," replied Leandro, dunking the bread in the coffee. "I have to sop this up like a kid. I'd like to eat something sweet today: a chocolate bar, maybe. I have one here that the switchboard operator gave me," he said, taking some chocolate out of his pocket. Removing the wrapper, he bit into it. He was always hungry.

"We're not playing today?" said Ronco, who was the youngest, with chapped lips.

"I'll bet on the guy in Room 10 for tonight," Urbino answered, caressing his chin.

"I'm not inspired. I want you to do a handwriting analysis for me," answered Leandro, showing him the folded pages.

Raco examined the pages, his hands trembling a bit. Apparently, he'd devoted himself to graphology and palm reading since childhood; to seduce women he would show off his talents by asking them for intimate letters, reading the lines on their hands so he could caress them, in passing, whenever possible.

"Hmmmm. . . . Not bad. Is she very young? Who is she?"

"I don't know. I found it on the street."

"So you want him to read the handwriting on a piece of trash?" said the bespectacled internist.

"What a jerk," Raco protested.

"I find the handwriting interesting."

"Introversion: the letters lean left," decreed Raco, "closed vowels."

"What does it mean?" Leandro asked.

"A person who rejects the influence of the outside world. So egocentric! Look at these flourishes in the shape of a hook. Narcissistic, aggressive."

"Who the heck is she? Spit it out already," said Mendiondo.

"I already told you, I found the pages on the street," Leandro answered.

"You've always had the same quirks. Do you remember that time when you fell in love with a voice over the telephone? You masturbated to it. You'd decided it belonged to a divine being who was fifteen years old but perverse, and you were going to devote your life to her. After three months you got the girl who owned the angelical voice to meet you. She made a date with you in a café. When you saw her arrive you had a fit. She looked just like your cousin, with a glass eye. Her clothes, her words, her face were all completely nauseating. People called her Cutie Pie."

Leandro told me that he took the pages as if he hadn't heard a thing and put them away in his pocket, that he left the room and headed for the white, dreary, endless corridors of the hospital. He told me the scene so vividly that I still think I saw him climb the marble stairs. His footsteps reverberated as he crossed dark courtyards: he peered into the rooms. At that moment he said to himself: *This profession is not for me, but what else would be better? What would be more interesting to me? Seeing people die horrifies me. Seeing cadavers disturbs me. The smell of the rooms of patients with contagious diseases nauseates me. And that unalterable place in my being where I fear contagion is growing. I would have to change my personality to keep doing this.* In one of the darker corridors he heard a woman's voice calling him by name. He looked everywhere to see where the voice was coming from. In one of the hallways he found the new shift nurse. She smelled of anise and had a gold tooth. Was she the new shift nurse that his cohorts found so enticing?

"Has a patient called for me?"

"The patients have never been so calm," the nurse answered, holding a syringe in her gloved hand.

"But, are you sure? I clearly heard an anxious voice calling out my name when I got to that door," said Leandro, pointing to a door that led to one of the operating rooms. "Maybe Irene called for me? Did she come in tonight?"

I drank in all that he confided to me. I hear his voice as if my brain were a recorder.

"It must be Miss Benzedrine," the nurse said, winking at him and biting her lip. "You're all the same: you always think someone is calling for you."

The nurse was in love with him too. At that moment he embraced her so as not to look at her face.

The taste of sea spray is how clouds taste. It's eight p.m. The sun has still not set. The sunset increases my anxiety. In any place at this hour I know that death exists: deaths, rather.

I wanted to sing the Brahms Requiem, but my voice cannot be heard. The wind censures my voice.

LEANDRO

For many years he was my obsession. It was as if he were several men. I see his face again. Leandro was handsome; some people said he was awful. His eyes were blue when he was confiding in me, blue like water when he'd make me suffer. Some days I noticed his teeth didn't look as good as I had imagined them the day before. Ah, the power of a man's voice! But I loved listening to him, even though or because he made me suffer. I can't forget how he told about that visit to the antique shop. The owner was one of its foremost antiques. Mrs. Arévalo, with her blond wig, joined eyebrows, and tiny mouth, was awful.

Any pain or annoyance does me good because it distracts me, snatches me from the great void.

"There was a lot of furniture all piled up together," he said, caressing me, "vanity tables without legs, a hodgepodge of objects, headless saints, old apothecary jars, clocks each marking a different time, chess pieces, music boxes, chandeliers, miniatures."

He looked at all the objects Mr. Arévalo showed him. I remember the exact words he used. I knew the shop and I knew its owners.

"But what are you looking for?" Mr. Arévalo asked, showing him an old crystal dessert dish.

"A souvenir for my mother. It doesn't have to be very expensive," Leandro answered.

"Here are some chess pieces. Does your mother play chess? They are display pieces. Does your mother have a glass cabinet where she keeps figurines and china?"

"Our house is very modest," Leandro mumbled.

"But even in the most modest houses they used to have cabinets. Your grandmother or great-grandmother didn't have a display case?"

"If they had one, it's not in my mother's house."

Mr. Arévalo was very tall and stooped when he walked. He had a woman's voice and a dog's face.

"Here you have a miniature and a candy dish," said Mr. Arévalo, opening a display case and removing a few objects.

"I like to tell you afterward about everything that happens to me," Leandro said to me.

Display cases are like the bottom of the sea. Why did I used to look at them so often? Did I have a premonition that some day I would be imprisoned in this water, as in a display case?

"How much is the candy dish?" he asked.

"A thousand pesos. Eight hundred for you."

"That's very expensive for me," said Leandro, shaking his head.

"Then don't ever go into antique shops," said Mr. Arévalo.

"I'm sorry to have bothered you."

At that moment, Verónica entered the shop through an interior door, and at the same time two luxuriously dressed ladies came in through the front door. Mr. Arévalo greeted them very ceremoniously.

"Were you looking for something?" Verónica asked Leandro.

"I'm too poor for these things. And it's almost my mother's birthday," replied Leandro.

"Didn't my father show you the famous clock with seventeenth-century figurines?"

"But it must cost a lot."

"I'll show it to you for the sake of curiosity."

While her father was attending to the ladies in the back of the shop, Verónica, with her silly face, was showing Leandro a strange clock and a little cage with a mechanical nightingale. You could see her legs all the way up to her bellybutton.

"What color are your eyes? The first day I saw you they seemed blue, but today, in the cold light these lamps give off, the blue has changed to violet, almost black. I've always paid attention to the eye color of people I've just met: the eyes and hands are the first thing I look at, what captivates me the most. Unless I know what the eyes and hands are like, I don't really feel that I know a person."

Why wasn't I Verónica?!

"Do you like it?" said Verónica, showing him the clock.

"I prefer the mechanical nightingale."

"I do too," said Verónica, winding it up. The nightingale moved its wings and sang. The song mysteriously repeated itself, and, upon winding down, its tone seemed erratic and infernally natural.

Where could I have heard it? At the bottom of the sea there are no nightingales.

"Can we get together some day?" asked Leandro in a whisper, and, when he didn't receive an answer, he persisted: "Where?"

"It's complicated. At the sweet shop on the corner of Quintana and Junín."

"What a slut," I exclaimed. Leandro didn't get angry.

"Across from La Recoleta?" said Leandro.

"Across from that huge rubber tree where they sell flowers for the dead."

"La Biela café? What time?" asked Leandro.

"At five. That's when I get off work."

"Your father didn't like me coming in here. I didn't know these things were so expensive."

"Everyone isn't obligated to know the prices here," said Verónica. "He's not angry; it's just his way. Look how he talks to those ladies."

"Doesn't seem like the same guy as before."

"He always acts like that when he talks to the ladies: it's one of his weaknesses, elegant ladies!"

What might mermaids be like? Horrible, beautiful, divine? I like to imagine them at night, but not now.

RODOLFA, NORAH, AND CEFERINA

Rodolfa, Norah, and Ceferina were women who worked at their sewing machines all day long; some of them were friends of mine.

Rodolfa was chubby and flabby, with a dreamy look in her eyes that could lead anyone down the garden path. Norah was dry, thin, and as angular as a man. Ceferina was tiny. Nobody liked her because she was a gossip.

The music on the radio was deafening in the crowded

little dress shop. There were two manikins; some women ran the sewing machines; others, with two or three pins between their lips, pieced garments together with long strands of white thread. I was there when Gabriela came in eating a hunk of bread. You couldn't tell if she was pulling the pieces off listlessly or ravenously.

"My mother isn't here?" she asked abruptly.

"What about your boyfriend?" asked a woman, as if she hadn't heard her. "Your boyfriend Cacho?" and, laughing, she added: "He's a peach."

"He's not my boyfriend," Gabriela answered.

"Oh, you've already moved on!" said another of the women, laughing raucously.

"Mother isn't here?" Gabriela persisted.

"No, dear. She's probably studying."

"Where?" asked Gabriela in frustration.

The women looked at one another. One of them winked, the other put her hand on her stomach.

"She's probably shopping," said the eldest, rolling her eyes.

Gabriela left with me but stayed outside the door to listen. It was one of her habits. For her, the world she listened to and imagined on the other side of doors was the real world. The other was merely a performance. "The things I'll hear today will be very important, maybe the most important things I've ever heard. My mother is a stranger. I have to find out who she is, what she does when she's not with me. And these dressmaker friends of hers will reveal the secret to me," poor Gabriela might have been thinking. The women inside continued talking.

"Imagine studying medicine while raising a daughter!

When she was a little girl she looked like San Gabriel, she herself said so. She was born March 18th."

"She wanders about with no supervision."

"She doesn't take care of her. Why did she even get married!"

"She makes sacrifices. She works all morning," the youngest one dared to say. "And Gabriela is a devil."

"Sacrifices?"

"Yes, even though it doesn't seem like it," the youngest one insisted, cutting a strand of thread with her teeth.

"She's a shameless hussy."

"She's nuts. I barely ever talk to her. She has photos of her lover in her purse, and a small revolver."

"No wonder Orlando jilted her."

"I don't want to hear about that guy: what a creep."

"Apparently, she carries the revolver to defend herself from sexual assaults. I don't know if it was the husband or the lover who gave it to her."

Rodolfa, who often defended Irene, put the clothes on the table and left the room. She found Gabriela listening behind the door. She patted her on the head and walked away.

Gabriela crossed the street with me. *I'll rummage through the whole closet. I have to see the photograph,* she thought. She entered the room. She opened the mirrored mahogany door of the armoire. On the lower shelves there were only shoes and piles of clothing. She climbed up on a chair to check out the upper shelves. She pulled things out and set them down on the chair where she was standing. I watched her. She found three purses, looked through them, and thought there was nothing in them, but in the black purse, in a side pocket with a zipper, she found a photo of a young man with straight hair and dark eyes. It was the photo of Leandro. She looked at it. She got down off the chair and, with loathing and excitement, went over to the window to see it better. She got back on the chair and found the little revolver. I took it out of her hands. I held it in mine, as if in a dream, caressing the cold barrel with my left hand. I put it back in its place. At that moment Irene arrived. She paused in the doorway and looked at us through the opening where the door stood slightly ajar. Then she rushed into the room.

"What are you doing?" she asked in an altered voice.

"I'm looking for something," answered Gabriela, startled.

"How dare you."

Gabriela, with the photograph in her hand, looked straight at her, defiantly.

"Give me that," said Irene, taking Gabriela by the arm.

Gabriela didn't answer her. She didn't have the slightest intention of returning the photograph. She pressed her lips together and looked at the ceiling, like a martyr riddled with arrows. Irene hit her helplessly. They locked in a struggle. In her desperation to recover the photo, Irene dug her nails into Gabriela's wrists, making her bleed. They rolled on the floor. I felt Irene's heart beat through Gabriela's breast; I felt the sweat from Gabriela's hair on Irene's breast. Without saying a word I left the room, ashamed.

Will I awaken the curiosity of the fish that rise to the surface? They come up at certain times and look at me, and I feel their fins brush against me. They think I'm the victim of a shipwreck.

ROBERTO RUSO

Roberto Ruso. A black child. The most beautiful little boy I ever knew. His ringlet curls and round face made him angelical. Leandro always had to tell me everything. That day he saw Roberto Ruso.

The children climbed on the horses and the lions. Three bears standing on their hind legs whirled on the roof of the carousal in the zoo. Leandro was waiting for Verónica, thinking that she had made a date with him in the most inconvenient and ridiculous place in Buenos Aires. He lit a cigarette and tried not to listen to the music. He went over to the llamas' cage, then to the eagles' cage. He was ashamed to be waiting. The date with Verónica had fallen through too many times for him to wait calmly for her now as if waiting for any old person. He bought some mints. Verónica arrived with a sketchpad and a pencil in her hand, as if she had been at the zoo all afternoon. When they shook hands they smiled, forgetting all the mix-ups. They sat on a bench near a bridge.

"I didn't know you sketched," said Leandro.

"I've been drawing for a long time. I studied at the National Academy."

"Let's see. Show me." Leandro tried to look at the page.

"Don't look," said Verónica, covering the drawing with her hand.

"Don't be like that. You're a font of knowledge: an artist and a pianist." Leandro continued respectfully, feeling inadequate: "How you tortured me. First we were supposed to meet in a sweet shop, then at the movies, and it's here at the zoo, the worst place in the world, where I've finally found you." He took out a pack of cigarettes and offered one to Verónica.

"I don't smoke," Verónica said, laughing.

"Does the smoke bother you?" Leandro said, hiding the cigarette.

"No," answered Verónica. "Anyway, it's more relaxing here. I love the merry-go-round music."

"You love it? You think this place is relaxing?" asked Leandro.

"Yes," replied Verónica. "I like innocent places. What did you want to tell me?" And she added, such an idiot, trying to seem indifferent: "I'm brimming with curiosity."

"I need to talk to you about your sister."

"I suspected as much," Verónica answered, flirting.

"What did you suspect?" Leandro asked.

"That you wanted to talk about my sister."

She struck me as a hypocrite.

"Does that bother you?"

"No."

"Shall we go somewhere else?' Leandro suggested. "Now that we're finally alone. Shall we go?" he added impatiently.

"To the wild animals' cage?"

"Do I seem so ferocious?" asked Leandro.

I remember it all as if I had been there.

"I don't know you that well, but you seem very impatient."

"I've been waiting to see you for I don't know how many days," Leandro said. "Don't I have a right to be impatient?"

"A week is not that long."

"It might seem that way to you. How about going to the lake in the park? Would that be okay?"

The two of them walked out of the zoo toward a motorcycle that was parked next to the gate.

"Let's go. Are you afraid to come with me?" Leandro asked, putting his hand on the handlebars.

"Afraid?" said Verónica. "Why?"

They both got on the motorcycle, and Leandro started it up with difficulty.

"I didn't you know you had a motorbike," said Verónica, settling listlessly onto the seat.

"I borrowed it," said Leandro, turning his head to look behind them.

"Watch the road," Verónica said. "We'll get into a crash out here."

"What did you say?" shouted Leandro, who could only hear the noise of the engine.

Verónica bent forward and said in his ear:

"We're going to get ourselves killed."

They made it to the lake, got off, and sat on the grass, under a tree.

"Don't you like it here? The lake is so blue: if we saw it in a photograph we'd think it was a lake in Nahuel Huapi, one of those where the water's so clear it looks fake."

"You're right," answered Verónica, gawking, "It's very pretty."

Leandro took the handwritten pages from his pocket.

"I've been carrying these pages around for a month in my wallet, or, rather, over my heart. I'm fed up with the people I know. These pages were the promise of something new. Do you recognize the handwriting?" he said, showing them to her.

"No."

"You're lying. It's your handwriting."

"So you know my handwriting better than I do?"

"I found this little notebook on the block where we live. I obsessed over the handwriting and the text for days. They're yours."

"And why would the handwriting and the text be mine? Do you know how many people live on that block who know how to write? Are you crazy?" Verónica asked.

"Don't torment me."

"But what does all this have to do with my sister, pray tell?"

"You'll see, but don't deny that this notebook is yours. I caught sight of you in the window the day I found it."

"Okay, if you're going to keep insisting, I won't deny it," Verónica answered. "What I'd like to know is why you didn't return it to me."

"I wasn't sure it was yours. I barely caught a glimpse of you in the window the day I found the notebook. Sometimes I thought I had dreamed it. These pages became very important to me. The word LEA revealed in part to whom they belonged to. I consulted a handwriting expert so that he could study the character of the writing."

"Those pages are very important to me and mean nothing to anyone else. They're from a novel I'm writing. I remember so clearly the day I lost them: it was the first day of spring, and I was worried. I was on the balcony sunbathing and writing, two things you can't do at the same time. The pages came loose from the notebook and blew away in the wind without my noticing. It wasn't until that night that I realized they were missing: I felt as if the air had become a person who would read and judge the most disgraceful part of my work, a kind of jury to which I had unwillingly submitted my book and that would never give me a prize."

"Is it about a crime?" Leandro asked.

"The protagonist has hated Lea since childhood. Ever since Cain and Abel, hatred has existed among brothers and sisters."

"And why did you choose the name of your sister for the character in your novel?" Leandro asked.

"Lea was not my sister's name," answered Verónica.

"Then why did all you call her that?"

"Because my parents liked the acronym that her initials formed more than her name, you must know this already."

"She never told me," said Leandro.

"I liked the name for a fictional character," Verónica continued, "because it was short and quick like its meaning: READ."

"From what I could see in four pages, the feelings the protagonist had for Lea herself were very ambiguous," said Leandro.

"Undoubtedly."

"But what's the plot about? Tell me, I'm dying of curiosity."

"It has no plot," answered Verónica.

"Can one write a novel without a plot?"

"Naturally. One could write forever about their feelings."

"As long as it's interesting or terrifying or moving."

Verónica and Leandro fell silent for a few minutes. Verónica pulled up blades of grass, and Leandro played with a small twig.

"It feels like I've known you for a long time. I trust you," murmured Verónica.

"You say that so I'll behave and live up to your trust."

"Maybe, but I don't know anything about you and you know all about my life."

"I know all about your life?"

"Well, at the very least you were my sister's friend, and people say that we look alike. Besides, you've been in my house, you've read part of my novel; let's face it, you know a lot, too much."

"Only by pure chance."

"You haven't told me anything."

"My life is banal and miserable and I have no talent. Have you been writing for a long time? Tell me the story again."

"It's very simple: the protagonist wishes for Lea's death. She thinks of killing her, but she's too cowardly to deal with actually carrying out a murder. The protagonist lives in a big house full of furniture and religion; she has to fight against a world that's very conventional. Night after night she plots the murder, like a female Hamlet. Destiny obeys her: Lea dies in the last chapter, but when she dies she doesn't disappear: she still weighs upon life, not like a shadow but as a live person, more alive perhaps than before. Her dresses, her recorded voice, her books and objects all remain in the house, and her dog waits for her under the bed. This leaves no room for remorse.

She, the protagonist, feels that she's committed a crime, but as the victim hasn't vanished, her anger toward her won't go away. Do you like it? Is it moving?"

"I think it's extraordinary."

"Let's not stay here," Verónica declared, seeing that it was growing dark.

The last rays of sun lit the tops of the trees, and a few soft, melancholy clouds stretched out in the sky.

"It's late," said Verónica.

Leandro, who was lying facedown, kissed her hand gently, leisurely.

"I don't ever want to leave here."

As she heard Leandro's voice, Verónica felt his moist lips moving over the back of her hand.

At that point in the story, I felt so wounded.

"But what were you going to tell me?" said Verónica, unsettled, withdrawing her hand. The idiotic woman doubtlessly thought: *He's in love with me, or all he wants is to have fun, maybe sleep with me, be my lover. He would have to have a lover.* Women are so conventional.

"I think you made me forget. Now I only want to talk about you."

Verónica listened to Leandro's voice, just the voice, stripped of all words or rather filled with other words, shining like aural acrobats. Women are so sentimental.

My waterproof watch wasn't working. What time was it? Four, five in the afternoon? On land I could always guess the time, but here I was disoriented by everything. A few meters away, on the surface of the blue water, I saw a long, dark line that looked like the body of a whale. I slowed the loud beating of my heart, so as not to communicate with the monster through the water. A slight dread paralyzed me. I threw my head back, closed my eyes, and floated on my back with apparent calm. Who was I kidding? Myself? Suddenly, in my fearful stupor, I felt something lightly touch my head. I opened my eyes. I closed them again as if this made it easier for me to concentrate on indifference. How far from indifference I was heading! Happily I was leaving hunger behind, the possibility of being hungry. Hunger distracts one from all other appetites. The slight brushing against my head continued to torture me. I kept my eyes closed until, touching what was brushing against me, I cried out: it was a raft. Although I never remember that word, in that moment I recognized in the terrifying form of the imagined whale a raft in all its glory. I stood up over the sea. Nobody will believe this, except Saint Christopher or the privileged survivor of a shipwreck who's approached in the middle of the ocean by a raft that asks for help, since it was the raft that was asking for help with its supply of provisions: grapes, peaches, and oranges, lovingly wrapped in fragrant paper and pretty straw, like boxes of toys. Thanks to the broken planks of the raft and its treasures I was able to climb up without difficulty. I didn't consider the possibility of spiders or snakes. I didn't hesitate: the smiling fruits called to me, so ripe that they were opening into two halves like mouths. The cling peaches in particular, with a rouge color that was the latest fashion.

Mirta Lamberti had an acrobatic type of beauty. On two white horses, doing a balancing act, she would have been a sight to admire. I met her in the Wings and Soles shoe store. We lived in the same neighborhood so that it was natural, inevitable even, that we would get to know each other.

Gabriela had been dreaming about her and about a pair of shoes for quite some time. Clothing was for her what toys and acrobatic beauties are for rich boys. Sitting on a chair in the shoe store, her foot propped on the stool in front of her, she looked at the shiny leather, the stiff shoestrings of the new shoe. Irene was talking to Mirta, looking at herself in a mirror, not paying attention to the salesman or to Gabriela or to me or to the shoes. I watched them.

"What could they be, those pages with that schoolgirl's handwriting?" sighed Irene.

"What pages?" said Mirta.

"Didn't I tell you he's going around with some pages in his pocket?" Irene exclaimed.

"I like these, Mama," said Gabriela, trying on the shoes. Her fidgety nose contradicted the sadness in her eyes.

Why was she sad? She knew they weren't going to buy her those fine shoes.

"How much do they cost?" Irene asked.

"Five hundred pesos," the salesman replied.

"Too expensive for me," said Irene. "Gabriel always chooses the most expensive ones. These are better," she said, taking a shoe out of a box and running her hand over it.

"Why are you so worried?" Mirta said to Irene. "You're suspicious of everything."

"It's an obsession," said Irene. "I didn't slept a wink all night."

"They hurt," said Gabriela, taking off the shoes.

"They hurt the first few days," said the salesman. "Then you get used to it—like everything."

Irene sat down.

"Do you have any sandals for me?" she asked.

"Coming right up, blondie. Don't move."

The salesman brought a pair of sandals and a pile of shoeboxes.

"Those are pretty," said Mirta, pointing to a shoe with her gloved hand.

"Latest fashion," said the salesman, taking the sandals out of the box. He sat astride a little bench to try them on her and said: "Polished nails. What pretty toenails."

"They bother me. They're uncomfortable." Irene went over to the display and looked at other shoes.

"Don't look at those, they're worse," said the salesman.

Irene sat down again; she, who was crazy about shoes, couldn't think about them. She wouldn't care if she went barefoot.

"Don't tell me you don't like them," said the salesman, sitting down again astride the bench and, caressing Irene's foot and placing it between his legs so he could try the shoe on her.

Irene must have felt the heat protruding through the material of his pants.

"The other day I saw you with some dark-haired guy on the street. When will it be my turn, sweetie?"

Irene took off the shoe and threw it at the man. Gabriela took off another shoe and threw it at him too. Irene, Gabriela, Mirta, and I left the store laughing. As we walked we came across a fruit stand.

"You're not going to buy me any shoes?" said Gabriela.

"We'll go downtown tomorrow, if I have time," she answered.

A man was playing a guitar on the front porch of his house. Gabriela, Irene, Mirta, and I stopped to listen. The man winked at Irene and looked at her breasts, singing:

> *Sleepy bye, when will I go sleepy bye 'n'*
> *lay my head upon your breasts? Sleepy bye. . . .*

"Let's go," said Irene to Gabriela. And addressing Mirta: "I can't go anywhere. I'm fed up. Always the same old crap."

"Why do you wear those bras?" said Mirta, who was the envious type.

"What's the matter with them? What do you mean?"

They stopped in front of a display window with mirrors on the sides, where they could see themselves reflected.

"Look at yourself," said Mirta, freshening her lipstick and pausing to look at her.

In the mirrors, Irene saw her breasts sticking out and smiled.

"What do you want me to do? That's how they are. They're natural."

Gabriela gave her mother a sidelong glance. There

was something sad in her face, reflected in the display window alongside colored pencils, notebooks, dolls, and a toy train painted green and red that nobody would ever buy. Gabriela wasn't sad about that. The charms and deceptions of the world were of a different order to her, she told me later. She felt very old, so old that she stooped over when she walked. Kicking a stone, with her hands in her pants pockets, she sighed like worried women sigh.

GUSANO

What was Gusano's real name? I never knew, or, rather, I knew that people called him Labardén after the name of the town where he was born. To describe him would be like describing a mysterious insect. He was hairy and swarthy, with eyes so black they seemed to have no irises; instead of speaking he would chew on his lips.

Gabriela loved Irene more than anyone else in the world. Nevertheless, she had spent the happiest days of her life far away from her—unforgettable days, in the countryside, in Labardén. Verónica, who taught drawing classes to the neighborhood children and considered Gabriela one of her best students, had taken her to spend the summer at El Cardal, her grandmother Chumbela's small country estate. There, Gabriela met Gusano and became his friend. "You'll end up crawling with lice," Chumbela would tell her, seeing them play together, but Gabriela even liked lice as long as they belonged to Gusano. Gusano the Worm lived in a hovel with a man who, presumably, was not his father. The man's name was Papero, and he made his living as a sheep thief and sometimes as a *papero*, a potato grower, but there was never a lack of food or laundry soap or shoes for Gusano. He was kind to Gabriela and would catch little birds for her: once he gave her a red-breasted finch. It was lovely with its red breast, but it didn't sing. Verónica tried to make Gabriela give the bird back to Papero, but Gabriela cried all day long. Verónica thought that birds were a bad omen. She was so superstitious that if she had bad luck while wearing a dress for the first time, she would never wear it again no matter how much she liked it. She would go back to wearing her old dresses, even though they were threadbare, if she thought they would bring her good luck. If she saw the new moon for the first time through glass, or if she broke a mirror, she wouldn't sleep all night long. Seeing a cross-eyed person on the street unsettled her so profoundly that she would go straight home. One day, a friend of Mrs. Arévalo's who came to visit with her eight-year-old daughter, who wore glasses because she was cross-eyed, occasioned a scene. The woman tried to show Verónica the beautiful color of her daughter's eyes, and she took the girl's glasses off so that Verónica could see them directly. Seeing the crossed eyes, Verónica covered her face with her hands, then ran out of the room, horror-stricken. That pitiful scene marked the end of Mrs. Arévalo's friendship with the girl's mother, who, outraged, left the house with her daughter in a huff.

Gabriela went bird hunting with Gusano. If Verónica had seen them, she would have forbidden it, but Gabriela skillfully hid her doings and pretended that she was fishing in the lagoon or gathering wild peaches in a distant pasture. To Gabriela, Gusano's life in that hovel without even a television seemed the happiest on earth. Horses and chickens ambled into the house as if they owned the place. That was the biggest draw for Gabriela. What better friends could she ask for?

No one forced Gusano to wash his hands or behind his ears, and the only baths he ever took were in the lagoon, in the rain when it rained, or in puddles where he'd stick his hands looking for his toys, which were ropes, wheels, wires, or old boards with which he built machines or cars. She would never forget the day they found an armadillo, or the ostrich egg, which they gave to the armadillo as a gift. The two of them would ride off through the pastures on a gimpy horse until they came to the lagoon. They would dismount, take off their clothes, and slip into the water. One night, Gabriela returned to the house so late that the next day Verónica grounded her and wouldn't let her out of her room for the entire day.

MR. AND MRS. ARÉVALO
Did they have faces? Tiny faces like rubber balls, that day.

Just like the salesroom, the dining room was crowded with furniture. It was a holiday. They were seated around the table: Mr. and Mrs. Arévalo; Inés, Verónica's aunt, who behaved in a flamboyant manner; Fernández, a history professor; Verónica; Alberto, a young student; Leandro and a woman in a feathered hat. Ceferina, a timid maid, served the table under the watchful eye of the lady of the house, who tried to smile at her guests. It was the first time that Leandro was attending such an intimate gathering at the Arévalos' house. Nervous, not knowing the relationships among the assembled guests, he looked from side to side trying to hide his discomfort. The meal was long—not even the soup course was missing—and the dishes that followed, so complicated with their additions of little salad bowls or tureens, prolonged the ritual. Leandro was relieved when the desserts arrived. The sound of people chewing toast exasperated him.

"Do go on explaining those theories to us, Professor; it's so pleasant to hear about something other than politics," said Mrs. Arévalo to the professor, who was seated next to her.

"That's very kind of you, Mrs. Arévalo," said the professor, slurping little sips of wine, a repugnant smile on his face.

"Now that truly is a work of art!" exclaimed the woman in the feathered hat as she served herself dessert.

What a dessert it must have been!

"It's my daughter's creation," said Mrs. Arévalo.

"I congratulate you, darling," said the woman, the feathers on her hat stirring as she turned to address Verónica.

Why doesn't she take off that hat? She must be wearing a wig that she's trying to hide, thought Leandro.

"Professor, do go on, please," coaxed Mrs. Arévalo.

"As I was saying," continued the professor, working his jaw, "ever since we have had recorded knowledge about civilizations, it has been proven that they evolve in cycles: while some populations are at the bottom. . . ."

Leandro deliberately dropped his napkin. As he picked it up, he saw that Alberto's and Verónica's feet were touching beneath the table so insistently that one of her shoes had come off.

". . . others are at the apex."

Leandro looked surreptitiously at Verónica and Alberto. He saw that they wore smooth gold rings. He had fallen in love with Verónica.

"Professor, will you have seconds?" inquired Mrs. Arévalo, indicating with her eyes to Ceferina that she should come around again with the platter bearing the mille-feuille.

"It has been observed," continued the professor, trying to help himself to the dessert from the platter that Ceferina was holding extremely high up, "that it is adversity that leads to the advancement. . . ."

Mrs. Arévalo gestured to Ceferina with a slight movement of her oystercatcher's head that she should lower the platter. The professor went on:

". . . or the decline of a civilization."

Still unable to cut the mille-feuille, he added: "This pastry is very hard to cut! Populations that must struggle against an adverse environment develop. . . ." He cut violently through the pastry, soiling the tablecloth. "Forgive me . . . they develop the strength to survive, and, using that momentum, they arrive at perfection, if we may speak of such a thing as perfection."

Mr. Arévalo, thinking about his most recent acquisition, a seventeenth-century clock with little figures that told the time, wasn't listening, although his upturned zebu cow's face appeared the very model of attentiveness. Ceferina slowly cleared the table.

"The same happens in biology," said Leandro. It was the first sentence he ventured to utter and just at the same moment a bit of dessert fell onto his pants.

"I've always said that suffering is a good thing,"

murmured Aunt Inés with a little laugh that sounded like a frog in her throat. "Why do we complain about bad governments? Afterward, the country rebounds, and we're on top of the world again."

"And why do sinners complain? Afterward, they atone and go to heaven," she added.

"Toynbee's theory is not original. It can be summed up in a proverb: every cloud has a silver lining," said Alberto.

The professor wasn't interested in the conversation when other people were speaking. Quickly, Leandro cleaned the spot with his napkin. The professor used his fingernail to sketch some drawings on the tablecloth. Mrs. Arévalo stood and spoke a few unintelligible words, and everyone followed her into the sitting room.

"What is this painting?" said the professor, pausing in front of a golden frame. The painting was deeply immersed in darkness.

"Attributed to Delacroix," replied Mr. Arévalo, coming out of his reverie. I found it in the most incredible place: in a hotel in Alta Gracia. At first, I couldn't tell what it depicted. I washed it with soap and this marvel appeared."

Mrs. Arévalo, Verónica's aunt and the woman with the feathered hat sat down in the armchairs.

"What a beautiful house! These old apartments are the best, with these high ceilings and large rooms," said the woman in the feathered hat.

"Give me a cigarette," Verónica said to Alberto, who patted his pockets and confirmed that he had none left.

"I'll go down to the corner store. There are never any cigarettes in this house," Alberto said, and left.

Verónica, facing Leandro, leaned her elbow on the piano as though about to have her picture taken. She was an idiot, as far as I was concerned, but I was careful not to say so.

"Do you still play the piano?" asked Leandro gravely.

"Not right now; we're in mourning, and Papa doesn't like it. Just for these first few days, that's all. My father is unconventional and always criticized people in mourning, but music brings back so many memories for him, and he told me he'd prefer not to remember."

"I'd like to speak with you alone," said Leandro in a low voice. "Could we meet tomorrow? Tell me where."

Verónica looked at Leandro in surprise.

"Why? What for?" she asked.

"I have something very important to tell you," replied Leandro. "I want to see you, but not here. We can't talk here. Where? Wherever. On the corner, at the ends of the earth."

"I don't know," answered Verónica. "Is it that urgent?"

"Extremely urgent. In a café, in a square, or in a movie theater?" asked Leandro.

"I don't go to the movies."

"Fine, in a café then."

"Fine," agreed Verónica, chewing the end of a pen, then added: "But which café?"

"América, El Águila, La Ideal. Somewhere in this neighborhood or somewhere else."

Verónica's father and the professor, who had been looking at the paintings in the sitting room, came over to look at one hanging over the piano: it was the portrait of Lea.

"She was too beautiful to live," commented the professor, "and what talent that girl had."

Verónica and Leandro's conversation was thus interrupted, and so they also looked at the portrait.

"Do you still study piano? Bach, Brahms, Bela Bartok, Hindemith, Prokofieff, Debussy, Ravel? Who do you prefer now?" the professor asked Verónica, leafing through the music books atop the piano.

"Prefer?" replied Verónica dryly. "I'm not allowed to prefer."

Poor little Verónica!

ALBERTO, JULIO, PERFECTO, CLODOMIRO

Alberto, Julio, Perfecto, Clodomiro: four filthy boys. I remember them as if they were my own brothers.

Those four boys gathered together at sundown in Plaza Intendente Seeber, where there's a ficus tree with very flexible branches. I used to go there sometimes to sit and read a book. The boys were doing dares, letting go of the highest branches to drop down to the lower branches, where they would swing like little monkeys. The four boys were friends of Gabriela.

"She doesn't want her to talk to us," the youngest one was saying, perched on one of the high branches.

"Who told you that?" said another boy, climbing down from the tree.

"Gabriela herself: she told her that we weren't a good influence because we're foul-mouthed boys," replied the eldest.

The boys left the tree and walked over to the bandstand. They started smoking and cursing. A group of students was dancing to rock and roll in the bandstand. One of the students was changing the records on a portable phonograph that sat on the ground. I watched them as if in a dream.

"We'll give her a scare," said the older boy. "Just wait and see what a good influence we are. What time did you say she comes by?"

The younger boy didn't answer.

"If you don't answer me, I'll bash your face in," the older boy insisted.

"Every Monday night at eight-thirty," the youngest boy mumbled, exhaling a mouthful of smoke.

"Who told you that?"

"I just know. I'm telling you. She's coming from an aunt's house."

"You hide behind that plant," said the boy. "And the rest of you? You guys get behind the hedge. When I whistle I'll throw her down on the ground, and then the rest of you come out."

The students stopped dancing. They gathered up the records, and one of them left with the phonograph. The boys took up their agreed-upon posts and went on smoking. Growing tired of waiting, they sat down on the ground. I thought I should say something to them, but they frightened me.

It was a damp evening; a light fog began to roll in, and the sun's glow was dying on the horizon. The streetlamps came on.

"Should we throw rocks at them?" said the youngest, looking at the lights.

"Let's do it," said the oldest.

I walked away sadly.

Beneath a grove of trees, the smoke from a bonfire mingled with the mist and the crackling of broken glass from the streetlamps. From the distance came the clicking sound of Irene's steps. I passed her. I didn't recognize her. Later she told me what happened. The older boy whistled. When Irene reached the front of the bandstand, the older boy appeared in front of her, covered her mouth with his hand, dragged her and threw her down on the grass. Irene struggled desperately. The older boy embraced her roughly and, pinning her arms, he looked her in the eye and asked:

"We're not a good influence on Gabriela?" Then he kissed her on the mouth and repeated the same sentence twice more.

The other boys surrounded them. They struggled with her. Irene was strong and managed to get free of the older boy's arms. She stood up. She saw a metal bar lying on the ground a few feet away. She picked it up and delivered a blow that appeared to injure the youngest boy. The boy fell to the ground. He seemed to have fainted. The other boys surrounded him. Irene, kneeling, listened to his chest and took his pulse, then went to find a water fountain. The boy opened one eye and closed it again, just as Irene returned with a wet handkerchief that she pressed to his forehead. Irene looked all around, ran to the edge of the road. The trotting of hooves and the sound of bells: a horse-drawn taxi was coming down the avenue.

"Let's go. We'll take him to the hospital," said Irene imperiously. She signaled to the driver to stop.

All together, they lifted the boy and put him into the

carriage. There was no one around. Occasionally, a car passed by with its headlights on. The sound of the bells and the horse's hooves echoed through the night. Irene looked at the boy, who was the same age as Gabriela. They boy opened one eye to look at her: Irene didn't notice. The boys elbowed one another: a sob, then another. Irene tried to identify which boy was crying, but they all had their heads turned away.

"Where to?" asked the coachman.

"To the Fernández Hospital," said Irene.

The carriage moved along Acevedo Street, running alongside the bars of the zoo, where the beasts could be heard roaring. Then, once again, silence, the trotting of the horse's hooves, and the bells. Again she heard a sort of sob. This time Irene realized that those noises that sounded like sobs were really muffled laughter. She saw the youngest boy's half-opened eye. Irene sat up straight in her seat and looked at the other boys in horror. Then she slowly began to cry, lacking the will to get down from the carriage. The boys looked at her in surprise. They stopped laughing and started arguing amongst themselves in rough voices. The carriage kept moving until it came to the Fernández Hospital. There it stopped.

Irene paid the coachman and walked away without a word.

Poor Irene. She didn't like the water. Sometimes we would go swimming in the river, but she almost always stayed on the bank. What would she think of the ocean, this ocean that surrounds me! She would have died a thousand times over already. There's too much water to cry. Wouldn't my eyes drown?

Rosina López, the corset maker, was also a good landlady. She had three chins and a streak of white hair. Enormous, she sat in a rocking chair, a smile on her impassive porcelain face. "Come in, come in," she said softly.

There was a party in the courtyard. Arranged on a large table covered in a white tablecloth were plates, glasses, trays of sandwiches and *alfajores*, bottles of cider, and pitchers of orangeade. The music coming from the radio was too loud. A few couples were dancing; others ate; others sat on chairs, fanning themselves or dabbing their foreheads with handkerchiefs. The nearness of summer could be felt in the sounds, the scents, in the demeanor of the guests. Irene and her friend stood in the doorway.

"I'm going to follow him one day, and if he's cheating on me I'll shoot him straight through the heart," said Irene.

"You talk big, but you couldn't kill a fly," replied her friend, stroking the doorframe.

"Or I'll find someone else; it's not so hard. After all, he's just a kid, and he has no money. I wash all his shirts and socks for him; I even wash his pajamas, and he never gives me anything, not even on my birthday."

"You've never cared before."

"I do now," declared Irene. "You'll see, I'm going to get some respect."

"How's the party?"

"See for yourself," replied Irene, looking inside at the courtyard. "Like any other family party they're serving chocolate milk, orangeade, cider, sandwiches, chocolate cake, and the worst part is I ate and drank a little of everything. The boys are worthless. I wouldn't give a cent for any of them."

"Who else do you like aside from Leandro?"

"Someone I could find attractive."

"But you don't find anyone attractive."

"It's not so easy. You don't just find the man of your dreams on any old street corner. But, God help me, it's at these sorts of parties where you find the least attractive boys in the world. Gabriel gets the most out of these parties. All she cares about is eating," she said, looking into the courtyard, where Gabriela was eating a piece of cake and pouring herself a glass of chocolate milk from a pitcher. "Why don't you go in?"

"They didn't invite me. Anyway, I'm a mess; I haven't shaved my legs, and I can't get rid of this stain on my shirt."

"Who cares? Existentialists are in fashion. That boy just winked at me. What do you think?"

"He's crazy about you. It's just his way of expressing himself."

Irene shrugged her shoulders.

"If he were good-looking I'd pay attention to him. Especially if he were intelligent, because you get tired of physical beauty when it doesn't come with something else."

Three gypsy women paused near the door. One of them was carrying a little boy in her arms, one appeared to be pregnant, and the third looked like a man dressed as a woman.

"How about some money to buy food, blondie?" said one of the gypsy women, looking toward the courtyard.

"We're starving to death, all we do is walk and walk," said the other, cracking her knuckles.

"Look at this," said the third woman, lifting her skirts one by one to display the varicose veins standing out on her legs.

"We'll give you something," said Irene, going into the courtyard with her friend.

They approached the landlady, sitting in her wicker chair.

"I've come in to say hello," the friend said timidly to the landlady.

The well-endowed landlady invited her to sit down, and a ripple went through part of the crowd like when a new hen enters a chicken coop.

"There are some gypsy women at the door asking for food, ma'am, and since we're all enjoying ourselves here we ought to show some compassion for the destitute," said Irene to the landlady.

"It is well known that gypsy women are the wealthiest people in the world," argued the landlady.

"They have varicose veins and children and they're hungry," replied Irene.

The landlady went into the kitchen with Irene.

"This meat is a bit past its prime, but it will do," she said, setting aside the meat, some bread and a sheet of newspaper.

"But it's bad for the liver!" protested Irene.

"So, you're a doctor now! Just imagine the livers gypsies have! Eskimos eat rotten meat, and it's good for them, sweetie."

"Let me wrap it up for them," said Irene, seeing the landlady's irritation.

The woman left the kitchen grumbling. Irene sniffed the meat, looked at it closely and then, picking it up with the tips of her fingers, tossed it in the garbage bin. She opened the refrigerator and quickly took out another piece of meat, wrapped it up, and, leaving the kitchen, handed the package to Gabriela.

"Give this package to the gypsy women out in the street. You hear? Go on."

Gabriela finished eating an *alfajor* cookie as though she were starving.

"Do you want to dance?" a boy asked Irene.

Gabriela turned around and studied the boy's face. She thought of the photograph she'd seen in her mother's wallet, but the only similarity she saw in the boy's face and the one in the photo was youth. Straining to hear her mother's reply, she took the package to the door where the gypsy women were waiting. The pregnant one took a deck of cards from a purse she wore beneath her fourth skirt and showed them to her, modulating her voice like a song.

"Would you like me to tell your fortune?" she said, laying the package on the ground. She smelled of wine. "I'll tell you if you're a good person or a bad person, if you'll win the lottery, if you'll receive toys as a gift: all for five pesos," she said, laying some cards out on the ground. "I'll tell you if you'll have a car, if you'll be a pilot or a doctor, if you'll travel by ship or in an airplane, if you'll have children, and if you'll marry twice."

Gabriela listened without answering.

The red-faced gypsy women looked toward the far end of the courtyard and, shrugging their shoulders, walked away.

"Ma'am, you forgot the package," shouted Gabriela.

The pregnant gypsy retraced her steps and said:

"We want money. What's in this package?" Without waiting for an answer, the gypsy opened the package and let the meat and bread fall to the sidewalk. She shrugged and declared: "We want money."

That night as I was leaving the party I tripped over a sticky bundle, and my heels, which were pointy as pins, got smeared with raw meat.

On land I walked a lot. Now the water envelops me completely, and my legs look like seaweed or feathers when they move.

There were lots of people milling around. They didn't talk: they looked at each other, sat down, walked away, and came back. Why were they all there? They were all very well dressed but in hues of green and brown, dark brown, Nile green. There were two or three young men. What a strange world! They gave me a salty drink; I drank reluctantly. I looked eagerly at what the world was offering up to me: arms that looked like branches, leaves that looked like hair, the color of faces varying according to the light shining on them. One of them, I don't know if it was a man or a woman (nowadays women wear their hair like men, and men wears theirs like women), approached me. I didn't care which it was. I always thought that as long as haircuts and hairstyles existed, I would know who I was

speaking to, but this time it didn't work. I spoke to someone who answered me: "You want to know my name? My
name is Pablo." And he sat down beside me on a sofa.
"These parties bore me." I replied: "I thought you were
a woman. Don't be offended." "I'm not offended. To the
contrary, I love being mistaken for a woman, but then they
realize that I'm intelligent." Emerging from my silence, I
asked him: "Are you?" He replied: "You'll see." We talked. He took my hand. "You have to hold hands when you
talk about intimate things. Spiritual communion is in the
palm of one's hands," and, squeezing my hand between
his, he said: "I believe in these things." It was getting dark,
and I closed my eyes. That was the moment when he kissed
me, but his tender lips barely touched me, and I told him
not to regret it. "I never regret anything," I told him, "it's
so lovely to discover someone new." "Where do you live?
Where can I find you? I'm tired," he told me and rested his
curly head on my chest. "How sad parties are! Don't you
agree?" "I do agree, but it's not so intolerable here since
I met you." "You're right, forgive me." I sensed the fad-
ing light. I looked around. What an unexpected encoun-
ter! Everyone had already left, and I was alone. The ship
moved. Would I remember Pablo's face? I looked at him
intensely, which led me to ask him: "Why are you looking
at me like that?" He thought for a while without speaking.
"I feel like we met a century ago." "It's true, and I meet so
few people like you, good people, so willing to be under-
standing." I took out a ring and gave it to him. "You won't
forget me?" Water filled his mouth. He couldn't answer.
At his side, I felt myself dying, and then he went away forever with his eyes closed, and I was almost dead.

The woman stopped looking at me. She was selling tickets at the box office. "You can come in to see the film, if you'd like. It's a story about jealousy." "I know jealousy so well," I replied. "Who doesn't? There's plenty of jealously to go around for everyone." Again silence. I was happy to think about someone at last: about Pablo. I held back tears so as not to cry in the ocean. Who can do it? You and I can. The tears ran freely, and I felt the same sensation taking over my soul. I think I kneeled, but I imagined it, and what I imagine becomes real, more real than reality.

The days race by. Sometimes I feel that life drags me off to other places like the water that surrounds me. I am not going to die. May my saint protect me, please God.

I am sitting in an unfamiliar garden. I'm asleep in a hammock, and I feel my memory abandoning me. I know beings that remember me, but I don't remember any of them. There are young people playing the most difficult games, but they aren't the ones I know, I saw them in important tournaments. My God, don't abandon me. I played tennis, sometimes; I won difficult tournaments, but now I'm not fit to win anything. I am looking at a vanishing world, the world that abandons me, that holds me in its arms and that I cannot restrain. The taste of the water burned my mouth, my God, when the water saved me. I'm afraid of being lost in this immense ocean. I don't know what to do so as not to die, so as not to fall apart, to lose my identity completely and forget everything else.

I walk on the ship's deck. I catch a chill, eat, get dizzy, today and tomorrow. I will be happy until the day of my death.

They called him Torcheli because he was twisted, one-eyed and crippled. Irene was afraid of him.

Irene advised Gabriela not to go to the zoo so often. Lots of men went there to look at the monkeys, men who looked like criminals, like Torcheli, thieves or perverts, for whom the sexual act required nothing more than a single condition: the perfect incongruity of the object of desire—a statue, an animal, a picture, or a child. Irene knew those men. She feared them, because they had shamed her when she was a child. She tried to scare Gabriela out of going to the zoo by telling her stories about animals that had escaped their cages. She told her that, at one time during her childhood, the merry-go-round had real animals rather than animals made of wood. One night, these real animals had usurped the strategic positions on the merry-go-round, upsetting the customary way of things for many years to come. The children's mothers and the owner of the merry-go-round didn't suspect a thing until a child became displeased with a lion, who bit her hand. After this, the zoo had to close its doors until order could be reestablished. Far from being frightened by this story, Gabriela became even more captivated by the animals. She stopped eating her dessert so that she could give it to the tiger the next day. She imagined a perfected version of the story her mother had told her. The zoo's architecture, its meandering paths, helped her imagination. The animals that used to occupy places on the merry-go-round were happy animals. The pavilions where they lived had little balconies where they could gaze at the stars at night. At any moment, they would return to the merry-go-round and bite and claw to pieces those sad wooden animals the children loved so much; they might eat the owner of the merry-go-round, and they would elect Gabriela to start it up and to choose the music: tangos, rumbas, marches, or boleros. Then Gabriela would be the only one to know the secret: Gabriela and the animals. Her picture would probably come out in the newspapers after a few years, when one of the lions, grown weary of an annoying little girl, would bite her, and Gabriela, seeing the crowd's terror, would shout *Don't be afraid, don't be afraid* to the animals, and she would spin around with them on the merry-go-round at the speed of an astronaut, to music and applause. No, she would never stop going to the zoo. She would never stop talking to the animals. She would never stop giving them a portion of her food. She had baptized some of the animals. Some came when she called them, others waved goodbye to her with their paws or wings, when they had wings. One of them bit her through the bars as she was giving him a cookie, and from that day forward she called him the Carnivorous Villain.

And to think how much I used to love swimming! Now I just float on top of the water, my name, my face, my identity forgotten. Sometimes I lift a hand out of the water to look at it. How strange a hand is. Sometimes I peer out over my toes.

GABRIELA

I remember many children, but none so well as Gabriela. Pale, her face the color of her hair, she stood out because of the seriousness of her gaze.

The only advantage of being a child is that time is doubly wide, like upholstery fabric. Time, of which there is not enough for anything, was as infinite as a desert for Gabriela. Whenever she had a free moment, and these were plentiful, she would go to the zoo. She liked animals because they behaved in a natural way: if they were hungry they ate nonstop, if they were thirsty they drank until they were full, if they were in heat they made love desperately, if they were tired they slept at any hour of the day, if they were furious they bit or scratched or killed their enemy. It is true that they also died, and dying is ridiculous, but they were so meticulous, so precise. (Gabriela would never forget her paternal grandfather's death, an apocryphal death.) Sometimes she would give the animals the cookies or chocolates she had been given. Sometimes she would put her hands through the bars to pet them. What could a jaguar, a wolf, a hyena, a tiger do to her? She was the animals' champion. She always carried a little notebook with her in which, after looking a them for a long while, she would draw them, carefully recording each of their names beneath the drawings, marking her favorites with a star and those she liked least with an x. In her opinion, the ones she liked the least generally resembled certain people.

This was the list of quadrupeds and birds she had recorded in her notebook, copying out the names:

- Zebu: sacred bull of India. *Bos Indicus*. Gray: Mr. Arévalo
- Somali Sheep: black head, white body: my grandmother

- Squirrel Monkey: black crown: Doctor Ernesto
- Collared Peccary: Tunga
- Spectacled Bear: cigarette and pill seller
- Syrian Brown Bear: shopkeeper
- White Oystercatcher: long yellow-orange beak: Mrs. Arévalo
- Silver Pheasant: my teacher
- Lady Amherst Pheasant: Leonor, the dead woman
- Seriema: Gusano
- Speckled Tiger Heron: my mother's dressmakers
- Great Horned Owl: Papero
- Paradise Crane: Verónica

If the animals had talked they probably would have uttered the same sentences as those people. Gabriela dreamed about those animals. Sometimes they saved her from grave dangers in an enormous ocean where she was drowning, or in a forest where other animals were chasing her, or in her house during a fire that would often haunt her dreams. She would wake up screaming and sitting up in bed. Sometimes, when her mother wasn't there, she'd get up in the dark and go out to the courtyard, gripped by a puzzling anguish. Gabriela's nocturnal anxieties worried Irene. At night, after what was almost always a frugal supper, she would make her cups of linden flower or chamomile tea to calm her nerves. But the linden and chamomile acted as stimulants in Gabriela's body. She began to suffer from insomnia, and the insomnia caused her to twist and turn in her bed like a worm. When Irene returned home after having been out for the evening, invariably upon opening the door she would become alarmed, thinking that Gabriela had escaped. She was buried under a pile of clothing, the sheets were tousled, the pillow was on the floor. Irene would spend a few anguished minutes inspecting the room: she couldn't get used to this daughter who waited for her with the sadness, perhaps, of children who sometimes wait for their parents when they don't know where they've gone, thinking that they've lost them forever, that they've been abandoned to a strange, cruel world. Gabriela at night was a sensitive, fussy, anxious child; Gabriela during the day was a happy, carefree, curious, independent child. One would have said that they were not the same little girl. Looking at her, Irene noticed physical differences caused by the day and the night. Sometimes she felt like the mother of two little girls. *Do the mothers of twins feel divided between two affections, like I do between nighttime Gabriela and daytime Gabriela?* she asked herself. She didn't know which one to like better: if the nighttime Gabriela who waited for her every night, awake—like a reproach under that pile of bedclothes—bothered her more, what reward was there in it for her to receive the hugs and tenderness she lavished upon her during those hours? The daytime Gabriela—on whom she spied surreptitiously, partially immersed in her life at school, her zoological research, her skill as an illustrator-decorator (she was a decorator of walls and trees), who exerted a fascination over her—didn't belong to her. She was an aloof, rebellious, sometimes malicious child, who tried coldly and methodically to discover what Irene did when she went out. A gossipy girl, perhaps, who could bring unpleasantness upon her because her irrepressible passion for talking might lead her to betray her mother in the most involuntarily cruel manner possible. Children are like that, Irene often thought, *for every small dose of happiness they give us, we have to swallow all the bitterness in the world. Men are like that too. That's how the world is. That's how Leandro probably is too.* She would pray as she had in her childhood, and she would confuse Gabriela's name with the Virgin's and Jesus.

How will they get me back onto the ship? Will they see me? Will they hear me? What will Leandro say? Am I in love? It's the only thing I think about, but I'm inhabited now by infinite people who disturb my memory. I'm living off other memories. Which one am I? Sometimes I can't find myself.

ROSINA DÍAZ

I wouldn't go so far as to say that Rosina Díaz was a good person. It was enough to see her face or to remember her wickedness for her to come to me on tiptoe, dressed in her usual attire, and breathe something into my ear: a malevolent secret. Nevertheless, she was so generous when pursuing whatever ends she'd set her mind to, rolling her dark, slanted eyes, that we would sometimes exclaim: "You're a saint, you're a saint." She was capable of being a saint in order to get what she wanted. Three curls shone on her mischievous little girl's forehead; her indistinct features were sweet. She was my schoolmate, and at the age of eight she explained to me the mysteries of birth and love, both of which caused me so much suffering.

Norberto, I have to think of the word "scrotum" to remember his last name. Doctor Descoto, director of the Private Eye Clinic, was tall and very thin, always hunched over as if passing through doorframes that were too low. In profile, his intent rabbit face was not as kind as it was head-on. When my grandmother had to have cataract surgery, she checked in to that clinic, and it was through that sad circumstance that I met Doctor Descoto. I associate his face with the countless patients wearing blue sunglasses who I saw filing through those rooms when I went to visit my grandmother, bringing the jars of candies and other sweets that my mother made for her. Doctor Norberto Descoto was everywhere, watching over his domain. In the main entrance hall, paintings, which all appeared to depict eye operations or blind people being led by children, angels, or dogs, charmed me. A little yellow statuette in the form of a blindfolded woman holding her hands out in front of her as if touching the air frightened me. One day I pulled a flower from the bunch of daffodils my mother was bringing as a gift for my grandmother and stealthily placed it between the little statue's fingers, thinking that I had committed an act of great daring, given Doctor Norberto Descoto's severe rabbit's profile, his eagle eyes with which he ceaselessly inspected the order of the house and the composure of his visitors. There, in those rooms, I discovered that the blind are seers, something that Doctor Descoto never knew. How did I discover it? I won't go into it now so as not to veer too far from my description. When he was talking, Doctor Descoto had the habit of caressing his chin and making a rotating motion with his shoulders, buttoning and un-buttoning his jacket. His quiet voice seemed to emit only secrets, even, or especially, when he talked about food. One day, Doctor Descoto was speaking so seriously to my mother that I thought my grandmother was about to go blind or that she was on the verge of death. When I moved closer, I heard that he was telling her about an osso buco and a mackerel prepared with white wine. I didn't know what osso buco or mackerel were, but I guessed that my grandmother's health wasn't hanging in the balance, and the mention of the white wine suggested that they were discussing culinary experiences. The gossips said that Doctor Descoto had two girlfriends, that he saw one on Saturdays and Sundays who was poor and blond, and another, who was a millionairess and brunette, whom he saw on Thursdays. I never saw them, but I know that they both wore glasses. Even worse gossips said that he masturbated, and that he had the two girlfriends to conceal his vices. Doctor Descoto was always busy running from one room to another, caressing his chin in front of every door. On one occasion he told my mother that he had also endured an eye operation, in that very clinic, and for that reason the statue of Saint Lucia in the entrance hall always had fresh flowers and a lit candle.

That's where I met Higinio Roque: he examined the depths of my eyes with a new ophthalmoscope. He looked like Raúl Ciro, but I didn't like him.

How horrible it would be to be blind. I wouldn't see the ship arrive or the seagulls or the storms.

Raúl Ciro! I never thought that I could like a person named Raúl. Black, brilliant eyes (they weren't black, they were chocolate-colored), a nose neither handsome nor ugly, a mouth with thick lips, prominent cheekbones, teeth that deserved to be extremely white but were blackish instead. As soon as I heard his voice, I was lost. I never looked closely at his ears; I really just imagined them. I never knew his age. I never saw his bare feet; I always saw him thoroughly dressed. In a similar fashion, I could have fallen in love with a photograph, and it was a photograph I fell in love with and not with Raúl Ciro, of whom I am not fond and of whom I have never been fond. What bad luck it is for those in love who fall in love with a false image! The imagined Raúl Ciro was the polar opposite of the real one. Red eyelids, disfigured mouth, blotchy skin, hairy nose, greasy hair, the height of a dog sitting down; all these physical details belong to the real Raúl Ciro. Silky black eyelashes, sensual mouth, coppery skin, the nose of a young animal, lustrous hair, slenderness, all of these physical attributes belong to the imagined Raúl Ciro. Nevertheless, I think his voice remained the same in reality as in the imagination, a warm voice that was always saying something different behind each ordinary phrase—a voice fit for a perfect face and hands.

Women love with their eyes closed, men with their eyes open, which is why I could love Raúl Ciro and he could not love me despite my considerable and very apparent charms. Poor Raúl Ciro! Few women will have loved him or will love him. He is no longer young, and he wants to be. His face is filling up with incongruous wrinkles because he rejects them. And what can his dark mouth that looks like a kidney or a foam hair curler possibly say? Inside each person there is both hell and heaven. Hell is easier to see.

Did I fall asleep on the raft? Did I fall off the raft? I'll never know. Please God, save me. I don't know where I am.

There were people in a place, talking; you could not hear what they said. There was an intolerable din. Among the bursts of laughter you could hear a voice like a clarinet that dominated all the other voices, deep as tombs. I'll never know what they were saying. Nor do I know if they were saying something or if the guttural sound of their voices was projecting some sort of announcement that everyone else in attendance understood. I dared to ask: "What language are they speaking?" The person I questioned looked me up and down; furious, I answered myself: "North Korean? Yiddish?" No one answered or protested. I left, my face wet and cold, in search of someplace silent. I threw myself on the floor like a used rag, aware that I was naked. A young man touched my breasts as he passed me. "Mermaid, go back to the sea," was the only thing I understood. This brought about an orgasm that I never want to repeat.

Thank you, God, for having made my life possible, for allowing me to write up until the last orgasm, and to have written this novel in your honor.

CELIA OR CLELIA

Her name was Celia or Clelia. She was a hairdresser at the Naiad Beauty Salon. Among swarms of faces, hers stands out for its ugliness. What use was it to her to be young? Her eyes, with pupils like pinpricks, peered out from beneath greasy hair, her prominent jaw ended in a double chin, her mouth was a twisted violet or purple slash. None of the youthful features she possessed made her even mildly attractive. She would do my hair without speaking to me, with her eyes fixed on my head. I would ask her:

"Celia or Clelia, what's wrong?"

She wouldn't answer. It was me something was wrong with. One day I had a sty in one eye, another day a boil on the nape of my neck, another day a cold sore on my lip, until my hair started falling out and I decided to consult a dermatologist, but the ointments and remedies he gave me were useless. My baldness progressed, my boils multiplied, and don't even get me started on the sties. Celia or Clelia would look at me sympathetically in the beauty shop mirror and, to console me, she would confide in me, her pinprick gaze fixed on the mirror, her frenzied, bitter voice trembling. Cooking was difficult for her, she told me: mayonnaise curdled on her, if she looked at the rice pudding the rice would separate from the milk, a cup of tea with milk underwent transformations under her gaze and became undrinkable. She couldn't open the refrigerator: a simple glance at the desserts or the ice cream would cause them to go bad; the same thing happened with flowers, but in that case it wasn't a matter of glances but, rather, of hands. The heat of her hands wilted everything they touched. In the mirror, I saw the tufts she yanked out as she combed my hair. Her eyes gleamed. Her hands moved like a harpist's when she would lay the comb aside in order to place invisible golden bobby pins among my curls, which she had set with beer.

"I have to go," I mumbled, watching the expressive to and fro of her hands.

"Impossible. I haven't finished," she protested.

"I don't feel well, miss."

"But you can't leave with your hair wet, one side hanging down and the other pinned up."

Trying not to look at her eyes in the mirror or at her horrible face or at the incessant movement of her hands, I staggered to my feet in order to demonstrate to her that I felt ill; and it was true that I felt ill: my ears were buzzing, my mouth was dry, chills ran up and down my body. Celia or Clelia's reddened hands brandished the hairnet that she wanted to put on my head, two bobby pins between her pressed lips glittered like monstrous teeth.

"Miss Clelia, I'll come back tomorrow. I feel like I'm going to faint today."

"You're just indisposed," she replied implacably. "Women's concerns. Sit down. I'll go get you a glass of water and an aspirin."

She took me by the arm and forced me to sit. The smell of shampoo, nail polish, hair dye, and heated cosmetics made me nauseated as I looked one last time, involuntarily, at Celia or Clelia's eyes. She disappeared behind a curtain in search of water and aspirin, and I took advantage of the chance to leave with my hair all wet, forgetting my perfumed comb that was so lovely! The one Remigio gave me.

I'm more comfortable faceup. Faceup I drown. Faceup

I look at the sky. Faceup I pray. Faceup I think about my entire life. Faceup I am my own bed.

REMIGIO LUNA

Remigio Luna, a mischievous but precocious child, would talk to me at the seashore like a grown man.

"I'll wait for you on the beach this afternoon. What time?"

How I would like to be at the seashore. Why can't I be an amphibian? The same thing would happen to me when I was sick in bed: I wish I were in bed, I would exclaim in my mind.

"I don't know," I would answer him.

"I'll wait for you anyway. Are you going to bring what you promised me?"

I had promised him a little boat. Remigio was thin and nervous. His eyes were green and a little bit sad. His thick hair fell over his eyes, his asymmetrical features. He was intelligent, sensitive. I could talk to him like an adult, and more cheerfully. He was eight years old; he sketched.

Love is like those Russian dolls that have other, similar dolls inside them that are not them, yet they are all one. Some men are happy because they have no family, others because they do. Remigio had no family. I was his family. One day he tried to rape me.

At the bottom of the ocean I want to discover the meaning of life before I die.

GILBERTA VALLE

Gilberta Valle was eighty years old plus two more that she wouldn't admit to. With her pink face she looked like a black skimmer bird. Small and thin, she was surprisingly agile. She lived in a village where we used to go shopping and on excursions to the hairdresser during the summer season. One day, the hairdresser Graciano Puco gave her a permanent: she, who never went to the hairdresser, had it done on a whim and also rouged her cheeks and applied lipstick for the first time, which really caught the hairdresser's attention.

"What a temptress you are, Miss Gilberta Valle!" exclaimed the hairdresser when he saw her with her hair curled. "Are you going to a party?"

"I'm going on a trip."

Gilberta Valle had sold everything she owned in order to go. She went every day to the home of Leonarda Cianculli, the secondhand clothes dealer. Leonarda, dressed in black, looked like a nun. Her green eyes twinkled sweetly. I met her at the pharmacy. She was always pregnant. By means of letters and photographs that came and went through Bahía Blanca, she had put Gilberta Valle in touch with a retiree who wanted to marry. Gilberta had sold everything she owned. She had her hair permed at the hairdresser's on the day of her departure.

When her hair was finished, she left in a hurry. It was a rainy day. The hairdresser wiped the steamy shop window with his hand and looked out to see where Gilberta Valle was going. He saw her go into the house across the street where the secondhand clothes dealer lived. She never came out again.

Three old ladies, as old as Gilberta Valle, who spent the day knitting, making sweets and chatting, intrigued by Gilberta Valle's disappearance, solved the mystery.

The secondhand clothes dealer, Leonarda Cianculli, and her husband began to seem suspicious. The couple had only lived a short while in that village, and they were poor as rats. Leonarda's husband bought damaged cigarettes, personally extracted his own teeth, ate meat and polenta twice a week, drank maté from an earthenware mug, never took his wife to the movies, and when she was ill he took her to a veterinarian.

Suddenly, the husband changed his habits. He ate meat every day, went to the dentist, the cinema, sipped maté from a gourd through a silver straw, bought packs of cigarettes every day, made soap, called a gynecologist. The three old ladies-turned-detectives, one of them pallid and the other two flushed, wondered where this wealth came from. They became friends with Leonarda in order to worm the truth out of her; they invited her to one of their houses, they offered her drinks, which she accepted until she was tipsy. Among other topics, Leonarda spoke of an excellent soap that she made for washing her body and her clothes, and, through giggles, she told about how she had invented the supposed fiancé, had handwritten the letters herself, furnished the photographs, robbed and killed Gilberta Valle with a hatchet. Then she told them how she had cut her into little pieces, which (mixed into the potash) were used (except the bones, which she buried) to make the soap.

The three detectives turned into the Three Fates, snipping the thread of Leonarda's life, since she died of unhappiness when she was arrested, a bar of soap in hand.

Will anyone think of me?

Where is my raft? I lost it.

MAURICIO CAIREL

Mauricio Cairel was languid and lively by turns; I didn't like his dreamy, elongated face. Many people are capable of admiring him, but people are crazy. "He's a great artist," they say of anyone who has an antiques shop or very long hair or black teeth and purple fingernails. He repulses me. He makes spiders out of iron and glass that he steals or buys from cemeteries. I had *café con leche* with him one afternoon in La Perla del Once Café.

ANI VLIS

I met Ani Vlis in a mirror upon surreptitiously entering a room in the house where she lived with her family. Small, thin, nicknamed Teru-teru, she was hideous, but sometimes in the mirror a flicker of beauty would gleam in her eyes or in her straight hair, in the incongruous shape of her jaw, in the studied tilt of her head. To see her as more beautiful, I would always look at her in any mirror there was in a room, if there was one, or reflected in the glass of windowpanes or paintings, and never directly, as I felt great affection for her, and, in my opinion, she didn't deserve to be so ugly.

At the age of seven an acute neurosis marked her for the rest of her life. No one could determine the origin of this neurosis, and the family came up with endless hypotheses in attempting to discover the cause of the affliction. Her parents were well-to-do and had showered her with toys as a child. In the display cabinet, two Scottish dolls, one with a drum, the other with a bagpipe, a gypsy woman with a tambourine, a chef with a toque and a skillet, a doll dressed for first communion, with rosary and prayer book, and a set of tiny furniture brought some measure of cheer to her life and amazed the guests, who would exclaim: "There's no one as happy as little Ani, who has so many toys." But Ani knew, ever since they had taken her appendix out, that each gift was a promise of a future torment. She remembered with horror those three consecutive days leading up to her surgery, when they had piled her room high with gifts. Why, if it wasn't her birthday or Christmas or the New Year or Easter or the day of her first communion, did they give her so many gifts? She grew more and more uneasy with the appearance of each new toy. The three nights arrived, promising something atrocious. Finally, one cold morning, without breakfast, they dressed her in thick, white woolen tights, took her from her home in a shabby taxi, and carried her to an operating room in a sanatorium. There was some discussion; then they tied her down, put a mask on her, and anesthetized her with chloroform. She didn't know where she was when she woke up. Ever since that day, poor Ani thought that all gifts were bribes, tricks, the promise of something horrible. She didn't want them and would cry when she saw them.

"I want to be poor, Mama," she would say to her mother.

But what was poverty? Poverty for her was to be free, to go barefoot, to not be operated on, to climb trees, to eat unripe fruit, to play in the mud and with fire, to not have a nanny or knitted gloves on her hands. Her mother replied:

"You don't know what it means to be poor."

Poor Ani would protest:

"I do know what it means to be poor."

"You wouldn't have any toys."

"Even better."

"Or shoes."

"I like to go barefoot," Ani would grumble.

LIVIO ROCA

He was tall, dark, and quiet. I never saw him laugh or hurry for any reason. His brown eyes never looked straight ahead. He wore a neckerchief tied around his throat and carried a cigarette between his lips. He was ageless. His name was Livio Roca, but people called him Deafellini because he pretended to be deaf. He was a loafer, but in his idle moments (he felt that doing nothing was not loafing) he repaired watches that he never returned to their owners. Whenever I could I'd escape and go visit Livio Roca. I met him on vacation, one day in January, when we went to spend the summer in Cachari. I was nine years old. He was always the poorest in his family, the most unfortunate, his relatives would say. He lived in a house that was like a railroad car. He loved Clemencia, perhaps his only consolation and also the talk of the town. The velvety nose, the cold ears, the curved neck, the short, soft fur, her obedience, all were reasons to love her. I understood him. At night, when he would unsaddle her, he would take his time saying goodbye to her, as if the heat coming off her sweaty body gave him life and took it away when he parted from her. He would give her water to drink in order to postpone the farewell, even if she wasn't thirsty. He dawdled leading her into the lean-to, so she could sleep there at night, beneath a roof, in the wintertime. He dawdled because he feared what happened next: people said he was mad, stark-raving mad. Tonga was the first to say it. Tonga, with her bitter face and pinprick eyes, dared to criticize him and Clemencia. He never forgave her for it, nor did she forgive him. I also loved Clemencia, in my own way.

In the attic was grandmother Indalecia Roca's silk robe. It was a sort of artifact that lay at the feet of a virgin painted green, with a broken foot. From time to time, Tonga and some other members of the family, or one guest or another, would add tacky flowers or little bundles of herbs that smelled of mint or sweet and brightly colored drinks. There were times when the moribund flame of a colorful spiral altar candle flickered at the virgin's feet, and drops of melted wax as large as buttons fell on the silk robe, adorning it more than sullying it. Time was erasing these rituals: the ceremonies gradually grew less frequent. Perhaps for this reason he dared to use the robe to make a hat for Clemencia (I helped him make it). I think that was the origin of his rift from the rest of the family. Tonga treated him like a pervert, and one of his brothers-in-law, who was a bricklayer, treated him like a drunk. He put up with the insults without defending himself. The insults didn't offend him at first, but after a few days they did.

He remembered nothing about his childhood except misery. According to what he told me while we were sewing the hat, he had scabies for nine months, conjunctivitis for another nine months. Perhaps all this contributed to his loss of confidence in any type of happiness for the rest of his life. At eighteen years old, after he began to court his cousin Malvina, he may have sensed disaster the moment he gave her the engagement ring. Instead of feeling happy, he was sad. They had grown up together: from the moment he decided to marry her he knew that their union would not prosper. Malvina's friends, who were numerous, spent their time embroidering initials onto sheets, tablecloths, nightshirts, but none of that lovingly embroidered cloth was ever used. Malvina died two days before the wedding. They dressed her as a bride and put her in the coffin with a bouquet of orange blossoms. Poor Livio couldn't look at her, but inside the darkness of his hands, in which he hid his eyes on the night of her wake, he offered her his fidelity with a gold ring. He never spoke to another woman, not even his cousins, who are ugly; he didn't look at actresses in magazines. They tried many times to find him a girlfriend. They would bring them over in the afternoons and sit them down in the little wicker chair: one was blond and wore glasses and people called her the little English girl; another was brunette with braided hair, and flirtatious; another, the most serious of them all, was a giantess, with a pinhead. It was no use. This was why he loved Clemencia so dearly, because women didn't count for him. But one night, one of those uncles who are always hanging around, a sneering laugh on his lips, wanted to punish him for the sacrilege he had committed with the grandmother's robe, and so he shot and killed Clemencia. The murderer's laughter could be heard mingling with Clemencia's whinnies.

How warm the water feels.

GENARO HASCOMB

Genaro Hascomb had the face of a rabbit. His blond eyes, the same color as his hair, seemed always uneasy. He always looked sideways and never straight ahead. His small mouth, with its thin lips, was always chewing a blade of grass, tobacco leaves, or a toothpick broken into three pieces. He was a farmer, skilled at growing tomatoes and lettuces. His last name led to misunderstandings.

"Genaro Hascomb. . . ."

Before the other person had finished the sentence my mother would interrupt:

"Where is he?"

"I don't know."

"Didn't you say he has come?" my mother would protest.

"I didn't say he has come," the other person would reply.

"Oh, Hascomb, the farmer," my mother would say. "I always forget his last name. I can't get used to these strange names."

In the end, the other person forgot the reason for mentioning Genaro Hascomb in the first place.

Genaro Hascomb worked on a farm where my mother bought vegetables. Genaro got sick and was on the verge of selling the farm, but he discovered a healer in Magdalena who cured him of his ills.

SARA CONTE

Sara Conte was of medium height. She seemed nice, and, though not pretty, she was attractive. She had a way of wrinkling her nose when she laughed that awakened a certain trust or tenderness in men. However, her nastiness soon peeked through: one day in an argument, another day because of some mishap, another because of jealousy or envy that someone aroused in her. Her victims would receive gifts. The first gifts were insignificant, but they soon became opulent, intolerably valuable. One day she gave Cacho a gold brooch. I warned Cacho:

"Be careful. Beware of Sara's gifts. She wants to conquer you."

I was right: she conquered him. She took possession of him.

In those days Sara had a Cadillac and would come by for Cacho at eight o'clock at night so they could drive around Palermo. There she would stop the car beneath a tree and kiss Cacho until she drove him mad: that's how she conquered him.

The water is cold; an Araucaria tree occupies my thoughts. Why, instead of people, do I only remember trees and some animal or other or a black dog that used to follow me? Now his eyes follow me, those loyal, feverish eyes. His name is Efigenio. He's being trained, he wears a training collar. I command him to bark, and he barks; to bite, and he bites; to lie down, he lies down; to leap, he leaps; to die, he dies. He does not like the ocean. Salt erases scents, stings the tongue.

Another tree memory: a chinaberry tree with purple flowers like perfumed daisies. The largest trees cover the horizon. Am I dying? If everything I'm seeing disappears, will I disappear too—and the animals and the water and the fear and the eyes and the murmuring of the waves and the wind, and this unwritten manuscript?

I'm going to die soon! If I die before I finish what I'm writing no one will remember me, not even the person I loved most in the world. Does this person exist? I believe he exists. He will never abandon me, and he will follow me like a divine shadow that I'll look for by my side, because everything that one looks for appears suddenly in the most unexpected way. I believe that love is a shared thing that never abandons us and that gratitude will exist as long as humankind exists. Life teaches us to be grateful, in one way or another. Within the greatest ingratitude, gratitude lies hidden.

I do not believe in the horrible guises of human beings, in bad people, in unjust people. There are moments when a perfect light illuminates them and they prefer to die at the feet of innocence or of intelligence. Either one of the two will be our salvation, even if no one believes this is so. In the seawater, I have drunk the beauty of the universe. All the animals gathered around me. They did not abandon me, except to join the plants in a perfect union, weaving love's last exhalations into unfathomable concerts. The crickets were the first to arrive. They sang with such insistence that I thought my eardrums would burst. But there are no crickets or fireflies at the bottom of the sea. Why did these miracles occur? Something in the world encouraged me to bring about miracles. I do not understand it. I only understand and feel fulfilled by the peace that it brings me. I scarcely feel the beating of my heart. Do I really have a heart? Or did I lose it in the seawater? Is my heart something invisible that will never be touched by anyone, that will not bear witness to my death? Who will answer my question? Who is there with a voice and wisdom to respond? It's better to cry when one is sad. But the seawater is salty like our tears; it would be better not to cry. It's enough for the ocean to mix its tears in with the waves and to carry us from place to place in the world.

These long days remind me of the city. Could the water, or coexistence with the water, be so similar to the rest of life? Today I walked to this garden that they call the zoological garden. The first thing I saw was a gazelle outside its cage. I approached it, I took it in my arms, caressed it. No person is as lovely as an animal. I have always thought this since the day I was born, and I think it today, more than any other day, because I feel lonely, and loneliness makes me feel tender. I hugged the gazelle and kissed her lovingly. But why did she allow me to hug her now, when she fled from me before? I raised my eyes and saw that she was looking at me, and that we were surrounded by a world of animals. Every animal in creation surrounded us in a circle: tigers, lions, horses, tortoises, elephants, snakes, spiders, cats, dogs; they spoke to one another, they complained, yawned, slept, ran around. Why was there not a single man, a single child, a single woman, either ugly or beautiful? I walked, dragged myself off in search of another world, far from the animals; I did not find it. The monkeys looked at me in surprise. They were so awful that I looked away, but they kept coming back, with their dark colors and their hairy pelts. I tried to talk to them. They did not understand me. I tried to play with them; they understood. I laughed. I think I laughed. They tried to imitate me, and they tried to speak. I did not understand what they were saying, but something in our eyes united us, and I tried to reveal the secret of my life to them. The water was cruel to me that day. I felt the cold again when I went under. One day, will I be able to live in the water?

A strange night, now without animals; I began to see the shapes of trees. I saw an enormous plant, it was an *aguari-bay*, the peppertree. I knelt at its feet and repeated its native name, *mullí*; I tasted its pepper-flavored leaves.

I saw a *pacará*, "Black man's ear," as my mother called it. There is a legend about this tree. Mother told it to me: An Indian waits for his lover. The ears of the tree continue to wait for her. She will never return, but the man keeps waiting for her in the ears of the tree, since neither the Indian nor the beloved return.